SECRETS OF MERCY HALL

Also by
Garth Edwards

For younger readers:
The Adventures of Titch & Mitch

For older readers:
THE THORN GATE TRILOGY

THE THORN GATE TRILOGY

BOOK TWO

SECRETS OF MERCY HALL

by
Garth Edwards

with illustrations by
Max Stasyuk

INSIDE
POCKET

Published in Great Britain by
Inside Pocket Publishing Limited

First published in Great Britain 2011
Text copyright © Garth Edwards 2011

A CIP catalogue record for this book is available from
the British Library

ISBN 978 0956 7122 5 7

Inside Pocket Publishing Limited Reg. No. 06580097

Printed and bound by CPI Group (UK) Ltd, Croydon, CR0 4YY

www.insidepocket.co.uk

CONTENTS

PROLOGUE

The crown on the pedestal glistened in the bright light. The eternal humming of the engine deep within the Dome was broken by the sound of footsteps.

A robed figure, stooped and wiry, mounted the steps and reached for the crown with crooked fingers.

Another robed figure, seated in a chair, took a deep breath. He had dreamed of this moment. This strange, hidden land, peopled by curious tribes, even more curious animals, and ruled by the Robes, the cruellest and wealthiest of them all, would be his. He was the biggest bully in a land of bullies.

'Now,' he thought, 'I will rule with an iron fist, until the time is right for me to leave... And when I do, I will take with me enormous wealth and be rich beyond anyone's wildest dreams...'

I

UNDER NEW MANAGEMENT

The jogging of the coach on the hard, rutted road made Milly feel drowsy.

As she dozed, she found herself reliving moments from her adventures in the land beyond the thorn hedge. Head lolling with the rolling carriage, she smiled to herself as she recalled the boat ride through the Rainbow Cave and the way the flashing lights had caused the incredible changes in her and her friends.

She was jerked back to reality when the coach and horses stopped at their destination: Hatton Garden, London.

Her companion, Robert, had opened the door and was now standing on the kerb side offering her his hand.

'Come on, Milly,' he said with a warm smile. 'We're here.'

He helped her out of the carriage and onto the pavement. The hustle and bustle of the city swelled around them in a great cloud of dust and sound. She was followed out of the carriage by a wolf-like dog, collared, but with no lead. Quickly, the three of them darted across the pavement and into the relative calm of a jeweller's shop.

A small bell tinkled as the door opened and shut behind them. Inside, stooped over his desk with a magnifying glass held to his left eye, was an old man with wispy, white hair and a thin, straggly beard on the end of his long, pointed chin. Perched on his forehead was a pair of wire-rimmed spectacles. For a long time he studied a diamond, held firmly in the grip of a pair of tweezers, before gently placing it inside a black, velvet drawstring bag and pulling the strings tight to close it. He finally looked up and, settling the spectacles back on his nose where they belonged, peered at the two people in front of him.

'Good morning!' he said, in a voice surprisingly powerful for such a small, thin man.

Robert Williams stared back and gave a weak smile. He was very nervous, and felt completely out of his depth.

The children at the Mercy Hall Orphanage had decided that because he was the oldest, it would be his job to travel to London to sell the diamonds they had brought back after their adventure beyond the thorn hedge. Now they planned to sell them to raise the money to buy Mercy Hall and run the orphanage themselves.

Robert had taken on the task willingly, but now he felt uncomfortable in his new suit; the stiff collar of his shirt rubbed his neck. Before the trip to the diamond merchants, George and Tom had taken Robert to the local tailor to prepare him for his mission. The stiff winged collar was the latest fashion for gentlemen in Victorian London; for

Robert to visit the wealthy diamond area of the big city, he had to look prosperous and wealthy himself.

He dug into the collar with a finger and pulled, hoping to ease his discomfort. It didn't help much.

'Good morning...' he said at last, though his throat was dry and the words came out more like a croak.

At his side stood Milly, dressed demurely in a flowered, cotton dress. She had a pretty, freckled face, short pigtails and her sharp eyes noticed everything. The dog sat obediently at her feet, though it too kept its eyes keenly on the man behind the counter.

'That's a nice looking dog you've got there,' said the man, staring down at the creature with a puzzled expression.

'Yes,' replied Robert, uncertain of what to say next. 'He's a...'

'Wolfhound!' said Milly quickly. 'Crossbreed.'

The old man raised his eyebrows.

'A crossbreed..?' he said, sucking his lips and nodding his head slowly. 'But you didn't come to see me about a dog...'

'No we didn't,' said Robert, finding his voice at last. From his waistcoat pocket, he pulled out a small leather bag and placed it on the counter. 'We came to see you about these...'

The mastermind of the trip had actually been Charlie Trinder, another of the children at Mercy Hall, who had lived as a homeless orphan on the streets of London for as long as he could remember.

It was after a brief encounter with the forces of law and order that he had ended up at the orphanage, only to be kidnapped to the land behind the thorn hedge, from where he'd been rescued by Milly and fellow orphans, George and Sam. It was in that same rescue that the children had found the diamonds. Charlie told them that diamond merchants had shops in Hatton Garden and they would trade diamonds with anyone who looked prosperous.

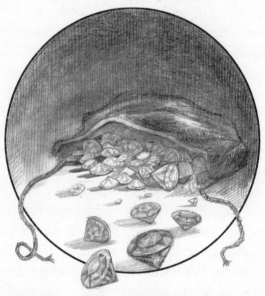

Nevertheless, it was a dangerous mission to travel to London with a small fortune in diamonds, so it was essential that a bodyguard should accompany Robert. The main candidates for this position were the three orphans who had travelled through the Rainbow Cave and been changed by the strange lights they found there. George had acquired the power to swim and breathe under water, and Sam had found that he could run faster than anyone in the whole world. Milly had been given great strength and could throw quite a punch when she needed to. For this reason, it was decided that Milly would accompany Robert as a bodyguard. At the very least, no one would ever suspect her of being capable of defending herself, let alone anyone else, and the element of surprise could be of great use to them in a spot of bother.

'Show the man the goods and look snooty,' Charlie had advised Robert. 'Tell him your father has sent you from South Africa to buy property and the first step is to convert the diamonds into cash. He doesn't really care where you got the diamonds from, all he wants to do is to buy them as cheaply as possible.'

'How do I know what a good price is?' Robert had asked.

'Sneer at his first offer, then tell him you want ten times as much or you'll go to another merchant. He's sure to cave after that and meet you half way, which should be about right. And keep tight hold of the money and the diamonds; London is full of pickpockets.'

As Hatton Garden had a large number of jewellers and diamond merchants, Robert and Milly decided to split the diamonds into small portions and go down the street selling them until they had all gone. If they took this long in each shop, it was going to be a tiring day.

The old man sniffed, put down his magnifying glass and wiped his brow with a grey looking cloth. Leaning back in his chair, he hooked his thumbs into his waistcoat. 'They're good. Nice and clear. Where did you get them?'

'An inheritance,' said Robert quickly. 'Are you interested?'

The old man smiled. 'I can give you five guineas a diamond, and that *is* a generous offer.'

Robert leaned forward and placed his hands on the counter, drumming his fingers lightly.

'My good sir,' he said, trying hard to hide the quiver in his voice. 'I have been assured that a diamond of that distinctly high quality is worth at least twice the price, if not more. If you're not willing to pay this, I shall simply take my business elsewhere.'

'Don't be hasty, young man, perhaps I could raise the price a little higher seeing as you've come such a long way. Please, take a seat. And the young lady too.'

Taking their places, Robert stiffened his back and tried to look snooty. 'Please don't insult my intelligence again, sir. My sister and I well know the value of diamonds.' He hoped his voice didn't reveal his nerves and was relieved to be sitting. At least that way he could prevent any shuddering in his knees.

It took another ten minutes of bargaining before a price of seven guineas a diamond was agreed and shaken upon. After taking their money and concealing it well inside Robert's jacket, Robert and Milly bid farewell to the old man and left the shop.

'You were brilliant,' enthused Milly, smiling up at him and linking her arm with his as they walked down the street towards the next jewellers.

'You certainly were most convincing,' added the dog striding alongside, 'though I'm not certain I'm a *Wolfhound Crossbreed*.'

'Drago, don't talk,' scolded Milly, looking around anxiously to see if anybody had noticed.

Drago was devoted to Milly, and she to him. They had first met when he had been pegged out for the Muttons and, after they'd helped him escape, he had stayed with the children ever since. On the other side of the hedge, a talking dog was quite normal. But in this world, it would be a very strange thing indeed, and could bring them all sorts of unwelcome attention.

Thankfully, no one in Hatton Garden was paying them the slightest bit of notice, and so, a few paces on, they stepped into the dimly lit establishment of Vernon & Jacobs, Diamond Merchants to the Gentry. This time they had more confidence and quickly obtained an even better price than before. By the time they reached the end of the street, their mission had been completed; all the diamonds had been changed into money.

'Come on,' said Milly. 'We must hurry before the coach leaves. I can't wait to get home.'

'Good idea,' said Robert, looking around. 'This

way, I think...'

The attack, when it came, was sudden and unexpected. It happened at the end of a cobbled street down which they had wandered on their way back to the coaching inn. One minute they were congratulating each other on selling all the diamonds and having enough money to buy the hall, and the next moment a ruffian dressed in torn trousers and a filthy sweater held a knife to Robert's throat and growled, 'Your money or I slit you from ear to ear, understand?'

Behind him another ruffian stood watch, glancing up and down the street to ensure nobody interfered with the robbery.

They ignored the slim, young girl who had been walking beside their victim. She was surely no threat to them, though the man was quick to realise the dog might be a risk.

'Jimmy!' he called to his mate. 'Take the dog out.'

This was his mistake. As the other thug advanced on Drago, pulling out a club from under his coat, Milly struck. Her well aimed punch lifted the villain off his feet and sent him flying backwards, where he crashed into his partner like a rock. Both men crumpled to the floor, gasping for breath.

More people were coming down the street now, and Milly could hear them telling each other what they'd seen.

'Let's get out of here,' said Milly, looking around anxiously at the people who were staring at her curiously. The scruffy unwashed crowd worried her and she wanted to escape before Drago became angry, doubled in size and drew even more unwanted attention.

Robert glanced at the crowd and, without a word, took off, running round the corner and away from the trouble. Milly and Drago followed rapidly. After a few more turns, they stopped running to make sure nobody was following them. Robert leant against a wall to catch his breath.

'That was close,' he said, wiping his mouth with the back of his hand. The money belt he wore around his waist was hot and uncomfortable but, as the contents were so important to the orphanage and the children, he simply smiled to himself, reassured that it was still there.

'It's not over yet,' said Milly. 'We need to be on the next coach home. Let's go.'

Back on a main road, they found themselves standing outside a large, terraced house with a black front door. As they were wondering where to turn next, the door suddenly flew open and a woman was pushed out. She stumbled down the steps to the pavement where she collapsed and sat down heavily. She was rather plump with rosy cheeks and had a grey bonnet tied over her round head. For a moment she just sat there and then, when she noticed Robert and Milly standing by her, she covered her face with her hands and burst into tears.

Immediately Milly rushed to her side and tried to

console her. 'Are you all right? What's happened?' she asked, offering the woman a hanky to wipe her tears away.

Before the woman could speak the door opened again and a man appeared. He wore a high collared suit with a matching top hat. His stern face held hard eyes, a sharp nose and sported a short, pointed beard.

'And take your brat with you!' he snarled and, pulling a young boy clutching a small suitcase from behind the door, he pushed him roughly down the steps as well.

'Hey, don't do that!' called out Robert. Normally a quiet, studious boy, Robert was not easily roused, but he was not going to stand by and watch a bully being cruel.

For a moment the man stared hard at him, then just snorted in contempt and slammed the door shut. Abruptly Milly ran up the steps and hammered on the door. 'You can't do that to people!' she shouted.

It was obviously a pointless gesture. Nobody came and the door remained firmly shut. Milly returned to console the sobbing woman and the now distraught boy.

A passer-by stopped and stared down as Milly tried to help the woman to her feet. It was a man in a frock coat with a tired, drawn face. He stood with his hands in his pocket and spoke to Robert.

'There's nothing you can do lad. That's Mavis Minchcombe and her boy Digby. The Holroyds used to live here and she was their housekeeper. They got into bad debt and had to leave the country. Now the bailiffs have the house and out she goes. It'll be the workhouse for them now.' He sniffed, shrugged his shoulders to show there was nothing more he could do about it and carried on walking.

'Are you all right?' asked Robert anxiously as Milly managed to help the woman to her feet.

'No, young sir, we're most certainly not. We have nowhere to go in the whole world. If the master was here he'd sort it all out, but him and Mrs Holroyd are in the West Indies and won't be back for months, if ever!' The woman blew her nose into the hanky and stifled a few sobs. 'Oh, what am I to do?'

Milly pulled Robert to one side. 'We can't let her go to the workhouse.' Milly was horrified at the prospect.

Robert understood. The workhouses of London had a dreadful reputation for cruelty and harsh conditions. Any adult who was unemployed and homeless was sent to the workhouse and any children they had were sent with them. Once inside, families were split up. There was one building for men, one for women and another room for the children. The work was unpaid and hard, the food was poor and everyone slept on straw mattresses on the floor. It was indeed a horrible place.

'She and Digby can come with us,' said Robert. 'When we get back and buy the hall with all this money, we could use a housekeeper and I'm sure Mrs Minchcombe will do nicely. Don't you agree?'

Milly smiled. 'I do,' she said gladly. 'And I'm

sure the others will too.'

'That's settled then.'

Mavis Minchcombe stopped crying and looked around. Then she looked down at Digby who was clutching his suitcase to his chest and realised that without Robert's offer of help she and her son would be doomed to live in the workhouse or simply starve in the street. Tears welled up in her eyes. 'We have nothing, only the clothes we're standing in.'

Robert gave a warm smile. 'And that's all you need for now,' he said.

'Come on then,' said Milly in an effort to cheer up the unhappy pair. 'We live out in the country in a far nicer house than this.'

'Are there any other children there?' asked Digby. He had curly, blond hair, an angelic face and, although his cheeks were stained by tears, he tried to smile at Milly.

'Children!' exclaimed Milly. 'I'll say there are children! There are lots of them.' Then turning to Mavis Minchcombe she added, 'Don't worry, I'll tell you all about the hall and the children on the journey home. But right now we have to hurry.'

It was a stroke of luck that the coach had two spare places, so Robert discreetly dipped into his money belt and paid the coachman the extra fares. The journey took several hours, which gave Milly plenty of time to explain to Mavis and Digby about the orphanage and how they were in charge.

To keep the story simple, she said a private

benefactor had made this possible with a generous donation. It was a story the children had all agreed on so as to keep their journey behind the hedge a secret. To pass the rest of the time, and to cheer up her new companions a little more, Milly told them all about the other children there, especially the twins Raffer and Agnes and all the tricks they got up to.

'But they are much better behaved now,' she added, so as not to alarm the new housekeeper before she even started her new job.

'And there's George,' she added, 'who is a brilliant swimmer and such a dear friend. And Sam who is the fastest runner in the whole world, but we are the only people who know that.'

Mavis smiled at Milly's descriptions, taking them to be the normal exaggerations of a young girl. She was not to know that George and Sam had received special powers when they passed through the Rainbow Cave on the other side of the hedge. Neither did Milly mention her own great strength which allowed her to fight off anything from street ruffians to crocodiles. Nor did she touch on the fact that Drago was a talking dog with his own power of strength. Instead she stuck to the easy facts.

'There's my brother Tom, who's older than me by two years. And his friend Ralph. Then of course there's Singer Smith, who has a beautiful voice; maybe she'll sing for us tonight when we get home.'

'That's enough names, dearie,' cried Mavis Minchcombe. 'You're making my poor head spin.

I'll never remember them all.'

As the last rays of daylight faded, the coach pulled to a stop at the end of a narrow, rutted path heavily overgrown with thick rhododendron bushes and patches of tall nettles.

'Mercy Hall!' the coachman cried in a gruff voice. 'Get off them who's mad enough to want to get off!'

As they climbed out of the coach, Milly could just see lights in the house twinkling through the leaves.

'Well,' she said with broad grin. 'Here we are!'

Mavis looked up the gloomy path and shivered.

'Oh my,' she said and, clutching her scarf around her neck and the boy to her side, followed Milly into the dark.

2

THE DISAPPEARANCE

For a while, peace and tranquillity descended on Mercy Hall.

Mavis Minchcombe was surprised to see so many children, and the children were very surprised to see her and Digby. However, they both settled in very well. It only took a few days for the new housekeeper to organise the children into a happy and thriving household. She quickly became a mother figure to the orphans and kept them busy by allocating chores and reducing the need to employ any further staff. Everyone was happy to chip in and do their bit, knowing that their survival depended on each and every one of them.

George was looked on as one of the senior residents of the household, even though only a year older than Milly, on account of his always seeming to know what to do in any situation. He went with Robert to Erringford, a small town only a short distance away, in order to arrange the purchase of the orphanage land and buildings as soon as they possibly could.

Their first stop was the Erringford branch of the Provincial Bank, where the bulk of the cash, packed neatly inside a brown, leather Gladstone bag, was deposited with the Chief Cashier.

Next, they went to see a solicitor. Robert explained that a number of respected business people from the City of London had formed a charity and donated the money to buy the land and buildings of Mercy Hall. The businessmen had specifically requested that all of them become joint owners and therefore would the lawyer please add all their names to the trust deed.

'Most unusual, I do declare...' said the fussy little man behind the desk.

Robert had grown in confidence after his trip to London and put on his most snooty look. 'My good man, if drawing up a simple document is beyond your competence, perhaps there is another lawyer in Erringford who could oblige?' He gave the man a narrow-eyed stare.

'No, no, it is not a problem, just give me a few more minutes to add the names,' said the solicitor, fumbling with his fountain pen.

George smiled at him pleasantly, but instead of giving the names of the businessmen, who didn't really exist, he handed over a list of all the children in the orphanage. The little man scribbled away and eventually presented the document. 'All you need to do now is to agree a price with the property agent and get these papers signed,' he said.

He smiled gratefully as Robert paid his fee in cash and departed on the most amicable terms.

The property agent, also resident in Erringford, frowned when Robert produced the document and offered to pay cash. However, after reading the document several times, and verifying an accompanying letter of merit from the bank with an associate, he grabbed Robert's hand and shook it vigorously to seal the deal. He also shook George's hand, just to be sure.

Robert and George were back at the orphanage for lunch with the deeds of the house and the news that all the children now owned the orphanage and the land upon which it stood in perpetuity.

'What does that mean?' asked little Elspeth, her legs kicking under the table with great excitement.

'It means for ever,' explained George. 'No one can take it away from us unless we choose to sell.'

'Which we'll never do!' added Robert with a clench of his fist.

George nodded in agreement.

'Well,' he said, clapping his hands together, 'any other matters to discuss?'

It was Mavis Minchcombe who stood up and raised her hand timidly.

'If you please, I've been thinking about learning,' she said. The children all frowned.

'Learning what?' asked George, certain that Mavis knew all she needed to know already.

'Anything!' she replied, and then, 'Everything! I mean, you're all clever little ones and no mistake, but you've got to keep learning or else you won't get any cleverer. See what I mean?'

'Indeed I do!' cried Robert, jumping to his feet. 'And I propose we engage a private tutor to teach us in every possible subject, especially mathematics and the sciences.'

'And the arts!' added Milly.

'And the humanities,' added Mavis. 'I've heard them spoken of as well.'

The rest of the children groaned at the thought of a tutor coming to teach them, but nevertheless it was agreed that Robert should appoint the right person as soon as possible. So it was that Miss Brackstone was engaged, on a generous weekly stipend, to attend the orphanage four days a week in order to teach the children everything she possibly could.

It was on the first day of teaching that Singer Smith discovered she'd been changed in the Rainbow Cave during their escape from the land behind the thorn hedge. On that memorable boat journey she had been fascinated by the changing lights overhead and had crawled out of the safety of the cabin to see what was happening. Later she crawled back again and nobody had noticed what she'd done, or knew what she'd seen.

Singer was a slight girl with a pale face, black eyes and long, black hair. She had a lovely smile and when she sang, everybody went quiet and listened in fascination to her beautiful voice. Nevertheless, she found learning difficult and came over very shy whenever asked a question by Miss Brackstone. Consequently, she made sure to sit at the very back of the class and sunk down into her chair, hoping to remain unnoticed.

But to no avail.

'Singer Smith,' called out Miss Brackstone from the front of the class as she was scratching shapes onto the blackboard with a stubby piece of white chalk. 'What are the defining features of a parallelogram?'

Singer shrank deeper into her chair, muttering to herself, 'I wish I was invisible...'

'Miss Smith!' called Miss Brackstone again, turning to face her pupils.

Reluctantly, Singer stood up. Before she even said anything, the teacher frowned and looked around the room in evident consternation.

'Where is Miss Smith?' she asked loudly, placing her hands on her hips. She wasn't the only one who couldn't see Singer, as all the children were now looking around in vain, despite the fact that they were looking right at her.

Puzzled by all this confusion, Singer raised her hand to speak. But as she raised it, she was astonished to find it wasn't where it was supposed to be. Neither was her other hand, nor, indeed, the rest of her.

'I'm invisible,' she said quietly. Sitting nearby, Milly must have heard something. She turned round sharply and stared at the empty space, then quickly took control of the situation.

'Miss Brackstone,' she said, turning back to the teacher, 'she was here a minute ago. Please may I have permission to leave the room and find her.'

'I suppose so,' replied Miss Brackstone. 'But if

you children can't be bothered to turn up, I fail to see the point in continuing...'.

With an apologetic smile, Milly hurried out of the room, leaving the door slightly ajar. Singer followed, taking great care not to brush into anyone as she passed. As she made for the door, Miss Brackstone continued the lesson.

'Parallelograms, Digby!'

As Digby mumbled his attempt at an answer, no one noticed the door shift slightly as Singer slipped out.

Outside the room, she found Milly waiting for her. Reaching out, she placed a gentle hand on Milly's shoulder, causing the other girl to jump.

'Singer?' she said to the air in front of her.

'Yes, it's me,' hissed Singer.

'What happened?' asked Milly and she put out a hand.

Singer took hold of it. 'I'm here, you can feel me but you can't see me.'

'How did you do that? asked Milly.

'I just said I wanted to be invisible, and now I am.'

'You've been changed,' breathed Milly, 'just like everyone who sees the lights in the cave.'

'I know,' said Singer. 'I'm afraid I didn't stay under the cover in the boat. I know I was told to, but I sneaked out to see all the different lights. But how do I get back to normal?'

'I don't know,' said Milly. 'Perhaps do the opposite of whatever you did before.'

'I want to be visible,' muttered Singer. Instantly she appeared in front of Milly.

'What a relief!' said Singer. 'But how exciting, I can make myself invisible.'

'And all you have to do is say it,' said Milly. 'That's amazing. Do it again.'

Singer looked around to make sure there was nobody else in the corridor and said quietly, 'Be invisible!' She faded away with a shimmer.

'Come back,' said Milly, who still held her hand. 'Be visible!'

Milly heard the words coming from the empty space in front of her and Singer reappeared.

Both of them laughed and, still holding hands returned to the classroom. 'I'm sorry, Miss,' said Singer to the teacher with a smile. 'I just nipped out for a minute.'

Miss Brackstone raised a quizzical eyebrow.

'Kindly ask permission in future.'

'Yes, Miss,' said Singer, and slipped quietly back to her seat.

Miss Brackstone took charge of the lesson once more.

'Now then, kindly take out your slates and copy down all the shapes from the blackboard, along with their names!'

When the school day was finally over, Milly took George and Sam to one side and explained Singer's discovery.

'Is she strong like you? asked Sam.

'Can she run like Sam? Or swim like me?' asked George.

Milly sniffed and said nothing. 'I might not tell you,' she teased. Her voice was mischievous and her eyes sparkled. 'You can just wait and find out for yourself!'

George stood with his hands on his hips and towered over Milly. 'Come on Milly, tell us. I don't like surprises.'

At that moment George received a hefty kick in his pants. He jerked forward with a surprised look on his face and turning round said, 'Who did that?'

Sam also whirled round, having received a slap on the back, but there was nobody behind him either.

A long gurgle of uncontrolled laughter came from Milly. 'Oh the look on your faces,' she said and could hardly speak for laughing.

'What's going on?' said Sam, bewildered.

George glared at Milly and at the same time received a tweak on his nose. Milly saw it twist right in front of her and promptly sank to the ground helpless with laughter.

Sam heard a giggle behind him, but when he turned round there was nobody there. Then out of empty space he heard Singer's voice. 'It's only me, watch!'

For a moment nothing happened, then Singer said, 'Be visible'. And suddenly the body of Singer Smith appeared, her face glowing with joy. 'I've been changed, see?' she announced happily. Then she added, 'Be invisible,' and with a shimmer, disappeared again.

'I'm still here, watch again.' They heard her call out, 'Be visible!' Again she appeared before them.

'Incredible,' stammered Sam.

'Unbelievable,' added George, 'and you've had this power since the journey through the Rainbow Cave?'

'I suppose,' said Singer. 'Though I only found out today.'

'I think you need to be careful with that power,' said George. 'People might not take kindly to being spied upon or having their bottoms kicked.'

'Oh, I know,' agreed Singer. 'I feel very uncomfortable being invisible. I shall only use it in emergencies and certainly not here in the home. In fact I'll keep it a secret. What do you think?'

'Good idea,' said Sam. 'But I'll bet it'll come in very handy before long.'

3

A PLANNED EXPEDITION

Six months later the orphanage was still a very happy place. Billy May, Ralph and Tom were busy preparing for their entry exams into higher places of learning. They all hoped to go to Oxford or Cambridge one day. Meanwhile, the younger children were settling in well to their lessons with Miss Brackstone.

Recently there had been some bad storms in the area, and a fair bit of damage had been done to the building's roofs. So much in fact that water now leaked into most of the dormitories whenever it rained. A few windows had been broken too, when some dead branches from an old oak had broken off and got blown against them. Now the wind whistled through rooms and corridors, bringing the cold air of an oncoming winter with it.

Robert, with his evident skill in mathematics, looked after the orphanage's financial affairs and, along with George, made sure that the whole place ran to order. But it was quite clear to him that with the way things were at present, they would soon have a problem.

'The basic facts of the matter are that we are running out of money,' explained Robert quietly to

George, with a frown across his forehead. 'We can take in more orphaned children, but the fees paid to us by the parish are pitifully small and won't be enough to maintain the buildings or carry out vital repairs. And of course there are the potential college fees to consider...'

'How long can we last?' asked George. 'I hadn't realised we were getting so low.'

'About six months,' said Robert with a grimace, and he looked at George. 'What can we do?'

George held his head in his hands for a while then looked up at Robert and said quietly, 'We have to go back behind the hedge. We know that's where diamonds can be found. We need to return and either buy some more or even find them ourselves.'

Robert shook his head. 'It's a terrible risk.'

George held out his hands. 'What other choice do we have?'

Robert bit his lip and finally nodded.

'Who do you think should go?'

'The older ones of course, but only if they want to. We can't force anyone to go.'

'Those who were changed have the best chance of success,' said Robert thoughtfully. 'And Drago of course; that dog is so devoted to Milly and the children I believe he would give his life to protect them.'

'We couldn't leave him behind,' agreed George, 'but as for the rest... Let's think about it for a while.'

Things came to a head that evening when Mavis Minchcombe returned from a shopping trip to Erringford. Looking flustered and anxious she hurried into the main room where the children were gathered. 'The Provincial Bank has collapsed!' she announced. 'It was terrible in town, a great crowd of people were outside the bank shouting and waving. I thought there'd be a riot!'

'You mean that big sandstone building on the corner?' asked Raffer looking puzzled. 'Always looked pretty solid to me.'

'No, silly, not the building. It means that the bank has lost all the peoples' money.' She looked anxiously at Robert. 'That's our bank, isn't it?'

Robert stood up, his face a deathly white. 'Everything we have is in that bank. Every last penny.'

Suddenly there was great commotion in the room as the realisation of their predicament sank in.

George took Robert by the arm and pulled him aside.

'There is no choice now,' he whispered. 'We will have to go back to the land behind the hedge sooner than planned.'

Robert nodded. 'Then we'd better start choosing some volunteers!'

'I volunteer,' said Charlie, appearing at Robert's elbow. He had seen them whispering and moved in closer to listen. The skinny street orphan was growing into an athletic boy, quick and nimble in his movements. George knew he would be good to have along and gave him a hearty pat on the back.

'I'll come too, of course,' added Robert, unwilling to be left out.

'No,' said George. 'You're needed here to keep an eye on things and handle the situation with the bank.'

'But..!' Robert was about to protest, though he could see George was right. He knew the finances and could deal with the legal papers; he really wasn't much good when it came to the dangerous stuff.

'Robert,' continued George, 'can you get Mrs Minchcombe and the younger ones out of here? I need to speak to the others.'

Robert nodded and quickly gathered together the younger children together. Along with Mrs Minchcombe, he bustled them out of the room with loud assertions that all would be well.

Once the door closed behind them, George turned to those remaining.

'We're going back,' he said firmly.

Milly was aghast.

'Do you mean... behind the hedge?

'It's the only way. I need volunteers.'

'I'm in,' said Milly, without hesitation.

'So are we!' shouted Agnes and Raffer together. If Charlie was going, then so were they.

'No,' said George. 'Brave as you are, I think those of us who have been changed should go. That is myself, Milly, Sam and Drago of course.'

The dog nodded heavily. George turned to look at Scorpio.

The little hunchback who came from the land behind the hedge, looked alarmed. 'Not me,' he groaned. 'If the Robes see me then I'm sure to be caught and pegged out.' He shuddered at the thought of the flesh-eating Muttons and began to shiver and shake. 'I can't go back again. I'll do anything... '

George looked at the small chap and frowned. He had no wish to take him back if he didn't want to go.

'And anyway,' continued Scorpio, 'if you're going back for diamonds, it's worse!'

'How so?' asked George.

'Where do you think diamonds come from?'

George shrugged. He looked at the others, but none of them knew for sure either.

'We found them in a drawer,' he said at last.

'Diamonds come from the NoGoodLands!' stammered Scorpio, his eyes wide with fright.

'Creatures there like you've never seen!'

'Enough!' snapped Drago, plunging the room into startled silence. With all eyes on him, he spoke quietly but with a firm and chilling tone.

'He's right. It's a bad place. I've never been there myself, but I have heard enough of it to know.'

The others looked at each other for any signs of doubt.

'But if we must go back,' continued the dog, 'then that is where we must go.'

'And how do we find these *no good lands*?' asked George

'The sign post,' said Milly suddenly, sounding quite excited. 'The sign post we saw when we left the Inn with Scorpio. It said *To the NoGoodLands.*'

George took a deep breath. 'Then we'll have to find the signpost and see where it leads us.'

Singer Smith put up her hand. 'I'm coming too,' she said quietly. 'My power will be useful.'

George nodded in agreement; she was young and frail but he had to admit her ability to become invisible would help keep her out of danger.

'We'll need to make plans. Those who are going, join me in the study. We will leave as soon as possible,' he announced, then realised that Sam wasn't in the room.

'Where's Sam?' he asked.

'He said he wasn't feeling too good earlier,' said Raffer. 'Went off to bed.'

George motioned to Charlie.

'Go and find Sam, see what the problem is.'

Charlie nodded and ran out of the room. The others retired to the study to make plans. A short while later Charlie rejoined them.

'Sam is sick,' he said with a sigh. 'Mrs Minchcombe thinks it's chicken pox.'

George's head dropped into his hands.

'Then it's just the five of us,' he groaned.

'Five is enough,' said Milly. 'And we've all got gifts, don't forget.'

'I haven't,' said Charlie. 'Not yet, anyway.'

'Yes, you have, Charlie,' said Singer, ruffling his hair. 'You've got more wits than most. That's a natural gift.'

George stood up and placed his hands firmly on the study desk.

'It's agreed then,' he said, looking at each face in turn. 'Pack what you need, as little as possible. We leave tomorrow morning.'

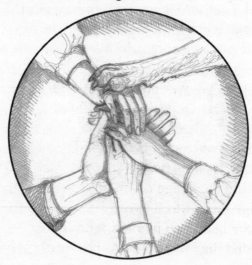

4

THE HEDGE REVISITED

It was a nervous group that set out in the early hours of the morning. The sun always shone in the land behind the hedge, so they'd packed accordingly. They were not prepared for the persistent rain that soaked them as they trudged along.

Each carried on their back a small sack stuffed with rye bread, some hard cheese and a few slices of smoked ham which they hoped would be enough to see them through any emergency. Milly had brought some extra rations of leftovers for Drago, wrapped in greaseproof paper. George also carried a small pocket knife and the remaining strip of leathers from their last trip; they were sure to have to pay for something at some point.

The great thorn hedge loomed over them as they walked, a great mass of tangled, impenetrable spikes. After returning from behind it six months earlier, George had deposited a large sandstone rock at the point where the hedge could be opened. Just above the rock there was a square branch; the trigger for making the hedge open up. On the other side of the hedge there was a similar square branch which the Robes had once marked with a post. However, the children had removed this post on their previous trip to ensure they could not be followed back to the orphanage

Drago was the first to discover the sandstone marker. The big dog had run ahead and scratched at a small mound under the hedge. Nettles and grass had grown around the stone and hidden it from view. When the group joined him, Drago jerked his nose at the square branch above the stone. 'There it is,' he said gravely.

'Here we go then,' said George, then he reached up and pulled on the square branch. A noise like a small groan came from inside the hedge, then a crackling sound built up to a crescendo and all at once the tangled branches started to straighten out. When the noise stopped, a passageway had opened up and they could see the sunshine lighting up the grassy meadow on the other side.

'Come on,' cried George. 'Let's get through before it closes.'

Brushing past droopy leaves and harmless thorns the friends darted between the vertical poles and gathered together on the other side. Standing back they watched the hedge close of its own accord. The crackling noise started again and in a few moments the hedge had returned to an impenetrable barrier.

George reached up to the square branch and tied an old yellow scarf around it. 'That will show us the way back,' he said, stepping back to ensure that the scarf was visible from a long way away. It was the only way the hedge could be opened and the only way back to their own world.

Charlie joined him and suggested, 'Just in case some curious passer-by decides to remove the scarf, I think a back up sign is needed.' He took a sharp stick from the edge of the hedge and scratched a large cross in the ground. 'That should do it,' he said. 'I'd hate to be stuck here for ever.'

Anxiously, they turned to look across the grassy meadow, but there was no sign of the Muttons. The creatures lived below ground and generally only came out in the evening. But they were also known to emerge if they heard anyone stamping or running on the ground above. Though they looked like sheep and moved slowly, tearing at the grass as they went, if a person got close enough to see their faces they would notice razor sharp triangular teeth set in a wide, thin mouth that gave the creatures a wicked looking grin. By that time, the Muttons would have surrounded the person and begun to close in. Once surrounded, there was no escape.

It was like walking from one season to another on account of the change from a cold, wet morning on one side of the hedge, to a warm, pleasant day on the other. As a result their spirits rose as they walked gently across the grassland towards the place they knew as Market Town. Here lived the Minlings, and Jangle, the warehouse keeper.

After about an hour Singer Smith started to sing, softly at first, then a bit louder, until her beautiful voice rang out across the meadow and the children all clapped when she finished.

'Come on Singer, let's have another song,' shouted Charlie enthusiastically.

She smiled and started a gentle, lilting lullaby. The children were so engrossed with the song as they trudged along, it was only when they stopped briefly to look at Market Town in the distance that George looked behind them.

'Oh no,' he cried. 'The Muttons are out.'

Whirling round they saw a line of white, woolly creatures following them.

'Run!' shrieked Milly.

Without hesitation they all started running towards Market Town. Within a few more minutes Muttons appeared in front of them and there was a danger they would be cut off.

'Stop,' screeched a voice from overhead.

George recognised the voice and, holding out his arms, motioned for the group to stop running. Above them hovered a bird that looked like a flying hamster. It had the large wings of a bat and a small furry body. As it flapped its wings they made a strange *tick-tock* noise.

'It's Batty!' exclaimed Milly and she waved to the bird they had saved from the Robes on their previous trip through the hedge.

Folding her wings, Batty dropped down and landed on George's head. She dug her claws into his hair to keep her balance and fluttered a few times before settling down. 'Don't run,' she said in her squeaky voice. 'It's the singing they want to hear. That girl has a beautiful voice and the Muttons like it. If she stops singing and you start running, they'll trap you like flies, and I'll lose some very good friends.'

They all looked at Singer, who took a deep breath and continued with the lullaby, though in a voice less clear than before. Anxiously, they looked around at the Muttons. They were still following, but more slowly.

'I told you!' said Batty in triumph. 'I was right, they want to listen to the song.'

'Keep singing,' said George to Singer, 'and we'll walk slowly to Market Town.'

The Muttons fell in behind them and when the grasslands ended, a great crowd of the creatures milled around in their wake.

'Well done,' whispered Batty, still perched on George's head. 'We should be safe now, they never come close to the river. Muttons can't swim!

'Let's head for the bridge just to be sure,' said

George, wincing as Batty's claws dug into his scalp.

'I hoped you'd come back,' said the cheerful bird. 'But why you would want to return here, I can't understand. It's not as if there's anybody here who likes you very much, apart from Jangle and myself of course...'

'Do you mind perching somewhere else?' asked George. 'You are getting rather heavy and your claws are sharp.'

'Flying is so tiring,' complained Batty, 'and I have to shout if I'm up there.' The bird looked at Drago. 'I see that big, ugly dog is still with you.' The Tick-Tock bird fluttered a few times and landed on the dog's back.

'He's not an ugly dog, he's beautiful,' protested Milly

'You can be useful at times,' said Drago to Batty as the bird settled down on his back. 'But you don't have to be so rude, and you talk too much. If you're not careful, I'll peg you out myself.'

Unlike the bigger creatures, Tick-Tock birds did not normally speak, but Batty had been through the Rainbow Cave and had been changed into a talking Tick-Tock bird. She was delighted with the change, but as Drago pointed out, she often talked too much.

'You'll do no such thing!' shrieked Batty, flying up into the air again.

'I'm so glad you found us,' said George, changing the subject. 'Can we stay with Jangle again?'

'Of course you can,' said the bird, flapping her wings excitedly. 'He'll be ever so pleased to see you!

The people in the land behind the Hedge were called Minlings. They were small with skinny arms and legs. Mostly they were friendly, but they were frightened of the Robes who ruled over them. Batty lived with Jangle, in the warehouse by the river. It was the Robes' depot when they came out from their valley, through the Rainbow Cave to trade goods.

Flapping her wings and tick-tocking away, Batty circled up into the air.

'I'll let him know you're coming and make sure everything is safe,' she cried, then flapping harder, rose higher into the sky and headed off towards the warehouse further up the river.

Arriving at the bridge, they looked back, relieved to see the Muttons had returned to the grasslands and were happily grazing. Crossing over the bridge, they passed some Minlings going about their business and nodded politely. The Minlings nodded back, but otherwise paid them no attention, which was a relief. The last time they were here, they had been chased along the river by an angry mob waving sticks and throwing stones. It occurred to George that perhaps Minlings had very short memories.

A few boats chugged up and down the river. Not too far ahead they saw the warehouse, a two-story building made of shining metal that glinted in the sunlight. As they reached it, Jangle came out to greet them. His arms and legs looked too long for his skinny body and he wore tight yellow shorts that exposed bony knees. The curly red hair on his head waved slightly in the gentle breeze. He wore a blue jacket over a yellow tunic, the uniform of a warehouse guard, and a ready smile on his narrow face.

Batty was perched on his head and greeted them again with a wave of her wings. 'Here they are again - the travellers from beyond the hedge!'

Jangle raised a hand and wagged a finger in front of Batty's face. 'Be quiet you wretched, noisy bird. How many times do I have to tell you?'

He reached forward and hugged Milly. 'I'm so glad to see you again. I was frightened that the Muttons had eaten you all. The last time I saw you, you were running away across the grasslands.'

'We're fine,' said George. Then he introduced Charlie Trinder and Singer Smith.

'That girl,' said Batty, 'has a lovely voice, and the Muttons liked it so much they let them through the grasslands *unmolested*! I've never seen anything like it before.'

'Any Robes here?' asked George, looking around for any signs of the hooded men.

'No, but they will be coming through the cave some time today. Batty is supposed to be keeping watch.' Jangle put his hand on his head so that Batty had to climb on to it or be pushed off. She fluttered her wings to keep her balance.

'I can't be in two places at once,' she complained. 'I saw the Muttons moving on the grasslands and when I flew over to see what had brought them out, I found this lot.'

'You did well, Batty,' said Jangle, 'but now, be a good Tick-Tock and go and keep watch. We don't want them turning up without warning. That would be a disaster for us all.' He was staring at Singer Smith as he spoke and she smiled sweetly at him. He smiled back, and couldn't help the slight flush that rose in his cheeks.

Batty flew up in the air and headed along the river towards the opening in the cliffs where the Robe's boat would appear.

'Come inside quickly,' said Jangle anxiously and he looked around to make sure nobody saw him usher them into the warehouse.

Once they were settled in the main room, Charlie asked if there were many Robes in Market Town.

'Oh yes,' replied Jangle, 'more than ever, and now they make Minling children work in the Dome. It's causing a lot of unrest, but there's nothing anyone can do. We Minlings don't like to go through the Rainbow Cave of our own free will. Oh, no, no, no, certainly not. I for one don't want to be changed.'

'I do,' responded Charlie. 'I want to be able to fight like Milly.'

Jangle stared at him as if he thought Charlie was quite mad. 'The Robes peg out anybody who has been changed,' he said, 'and not all changes are good. It's very dangerous to go through the Rainbow Cave.'

'Well, we have no choice,' interrupted George. 'There are diamonds on the other side, and we have to find them. Unfortunately, all we know is that they may be found in the NoGoodLands.'

Jangle sighed. 'Indeed they are, and if you want to go there, you're even madder than I thought.' He leaned closer and began to whisper, as though conspiring in some plot.

'I hear the Robes talk when they stay here. They say there is a new King of the Robes. He is a very big, cruel person and he wants to have any sparkling stones people can find. I have heard the Robes say that the Waterlanders have diamonds by the million and the King has sent groups of Robes into the NoGoodLands to bring them back, but they never return. They just disappear.

'Where do the Waterlanders live?' asked Milly.

'Somewhere on the other side of the NoGoodLands, but to get there they have to pass through the swamps, and Robes have always been frightened of the people who live in the swamps.'

'Well, we know there is a signpost to the NoGoodLands on the way to the Dome, because we saw it,' said Milly. 'So we get to the signpost and walk, or we find some horses to ride.'

'Or take one of the strange carts the Robes use,' suggested Singer.

Jangle shook his head. 'Magneto carts won't work in the swamps, and I doubt any horse would want to go there. I hear it's not an easy place to travel in. It's infested with all sorts of horrible creatures; no doubt they're the reason the Robes disappear...'

'There may be an easier way to get there,' said

Charlie thoughtfully. 'I saw some people once, when I was in the Dome. They had green skin!'

Jangle nodded. 'That's them,' he said. 'They're the Waterlanders.'

'They came to sell diamonds, I'm sure of it. They were in this long, narrow boat.'

'A canoe,' said George looking pleased. 'Of course! We don't have to walk. If the Waterlanders were in a canoe then they must have reached the Dome by travelling along the river. The same river as here, right outside the warehouse door. It goes through the Rainbow Cave, into the Robes' land, and we know it flows in a great curve to the Dome. We can go by boat and see how far we get.'

Milly clapped her hands. 'That's right,' she said. 'We don't have to walk.' She smiled nicely at Jangle and added, 'Can you find us a boat?'

Before Jangle could answer, Batty returned and flew in through the open window so fast that she crashed into the opposite wall.

'Yow!' was all she said, before sliding down the wall and landing in a heap on the floor with her wings stretched out.

Jangle rushed over and gently lifted her onto the table. 'Batty? Are you all right? Say something!' His voice was full of concern for his little friend.

It was several minutes before Batty stirred and raised her head. 'What happened?' she whispered.

'You flew so fast you couldn't stop, you silly bird,' said Jangle.

Urgently, Batty pushed herself upright using her

wings. 'That's right, the Robes are here! King Robe himself is here,' she shouted in agitation. 'In a big boat and going very fast. Must warn Jangle.'

Milly rushed to the window and looked out. 'They're right outside,' she hissed. 'We must run. Jangle, where's the back door?'

'There isn't one,' shouted Jangle. 'You'll have to go out the front, but tie me up first. If the Robes know I've helped you they will peg me out for the Muttons. I don't want to be eaten.'

'We need some rope,' said George looking round the room.

Jangle dashed over to a box in the corner and brought out a ball of string. Rapidly, George tied the Minling's wrists and legs together, wished him luck and followed his friends out of the warehouse.

The Robes' boat was pulling into the quay. Standing in the prow, a big man in an orange gown had pulled off his hood and was adjusting the gold, diamond encrusted crown that sat on top of his head. The crown was obviously a symbol of his rank and power, but it was not the scintillating brilliance of the headgear that stopped them in their tracks, it was the face of the Robe that wore it.

Eyes like black buttons stared out of a blotched, red face. It was fatter than when they had last seen it with great jowls sagging down on either side of the chin, but it was still the face of Old Barking Mad, the former head of the Mercy Hall Home for Displaced Children.

The children stared in horror at the huge man,

who seemed bigger than ever, and who now stared back at them in shocked surprise.

'You...' he hissed, raising a finger.

'Yes,' said George. 'What a surprise...'

Jethro Barking was in no mood for pleasantries.

'Seize them!' he screamed suddenly, his face turning red with rage.

Immediately five Robes leapt off the boat to carry out his orders. The friends turned to flee but found another squad of Robes hurrying along the path to meet their king. Their escape route was blocked. There was no other option but to fight their way out.

Milly turned and punched a Robe from the boat who had both his arms outstretched to grab her. He fell backwards with a crash and stayed down, dazed. Drago grew in size, his legs stiffened and his eyes turned red with anger. His precious Milly was being attacked and he was ready to fight anyone. With a snarl he launched himself at the Robes who now surrounded them. One Robe was knocked backwards with the force of Drago's charge, but for a moment the dog was off balance. Seeing their chance, two Robes carrying poles, charged at Drago. Before he could regain his balance, the Robes pushed the dog into the river.

Two more Robes grabbed George and, although he fought fiercely, he was no match for them and ended up on the ground with both his assailants pinning him down.

The slim and agile Charlie nearly escaped. He'd wriggled out of the grasp of one Robe, danced past another, darted between the legs of a third and then pushed a fourth Robe into the river. Unfortunately, he hesitated just when he was free. At that moment a Robe grabbed him with both arms and heaved him off the ground. Charlie kicked and struggled with all his might but he couldn't break the tight hold around his chest, and soon found himself struggling for breath.

Beneath a pile of Robes, Milly could not be seen. Her change in the Rainbow Cave had given her great strength, but it was not enough to overcome all the Robes who'd charged at her. She lay on the ground completely covered by the bodies of five Robes as they pinned her down and tried to bind her with cords of rope.

The fight had been fierce but brief. Overhead, Batty hovered, making frantic tick-tock noises and hurling advice down at the fighters. 'Hit them harder Milly!' she shouted. 'Go Charlie, run! All Robes are useless dunderheads!' she screamed in anger. The agitated bird suddenly folded her wings together and dropped like a stone. Her target was the leader of the Robes who stood sneering on the quayside watching his men gain the upper hand. Batty hit the head of the king with a thump and, with her claws outstretched she scrabbled furiously at his head. Tufts of hair flew everywhere and before the king could react, Batty flew away screaming furiously. In her claws she carried the crown that Jethro Barking had just placed on his head.

From his very squashed position under the

Robes, George saw what happened and grinned as he watched Batty swoop down again, screeching in triumph in order to dangle the crown just out of everyone's reach.

'Let my friends go or I'll drop the crown in the river,' she shouted.

'Bring it back, or I'll chop them into little pieces,' howled the king in a rage, his face contorted and his eyes popping out of his head.

George stared at his old headmaster and realised that Jethro Barking was now quite mad.

Ropes were secured and George, Milly and Charlie were now firmly tied together. The alarm was well and truly raised and a pair of Robes on the shore chased Drago down the river and poked him with poles if he tried to clamber up the bank.

Batty had turned her attentions to Drago and, still carrying the crown, she now hovered over the dog and shouted down at the Robes who were determined that the dangerous creature should drown. 'Leave him alone,' she shouted. 'Go back, the king needs you, he's lost his head and he wants you to find it,' she cackled at her own humour and tried to dive bomb the Robes. But with the crown firmly clutched in her claws she wasn't very effective.

Meanwhile, the King of the Robes turned his attention to the helpless children.

'Where is the square branch?' he snarled. Then without waiting for an answer, he turned to the Robes and shouted, 'One of them is missing. There were two girls a minute ago. You've let one escape!

Keep *them* in the warehouse, find that girl and kill that wretched *dog*! And get my crown back!' His voice rose in a crescendo and all but two of the Robes hurried away to do his bidding.

Singer Smith had made herself invisible but stayed on the quayside. She was frightened, her lips trembled, her legs were shaking and she didn't know what to do. However, when Batty flew off to help Drago, she realised that she must help the dog first.

Hurrying along the path by the river she caught up with the Robes who were poking Drago with sticks and making him float helplessly with the current. She ran swiftly past them and looked desperately for some way of helping. A boat or a raft or anything that would float was what she wanted, but nothing could be found. Looking up she saw Batty. 'Help me, Batty. Over here.'

The Tick-Tock bird heard the voice, recognised it and flew in its direction. Singer made herself become visible just long enough to give Batty an enormous shock and to tell her how to save Drago. The bird flew off again and, moments later, Singer saw her fluttering further down the bank of the river. She raced towards Batty who had spotted an old tree trunk and, when the invisible girl reached it, the bird screeched with delight.

'Go on Singer, push it in the river. I'll go and tell Drago.'

Singer pushed with a strength born of desperation

and slowly the tree trunk floated out onto the water. She then waded out into the river and, holding tightly to stop it floating away, waited for Drago to reach her.

The desperate dog was drowning slowly. Although he could paddle frantically with his paws, he was tiring rapidly and choking as the water kept splashing over him. Batty had told him to swim for the log before the Robes saw it floating in the river and, taking a deep breath, the frightened dog allowed the river to carry him along.

Singer saw him coming and called out his name. 'Quickly Drago, grab the log!'

A branch jutted out from the end of the tree trunk and as the water swept him towards it he opened his mouth and bit it firmly. At the same time Singer lost her grip on the other end and immediately the dog and the log were swept out to the middle of the river.

The Robes reached the point where Singer stood in the water up to her waist. She remained standing perfectly still, too frightened to move in case the Robes became aware of her invisible presence. But the orange gowned men were too busy shouting and shaking their fists at the dog to notice. When the Robes gave up the chase and left the river bank she turned round anxiously to look for Drago.

The dog had managed to climb onto the great log and, although he looked very unsteady, she was relieved to see Batty flying over him shouting words of encouragement. Dripping wet, the invisible girl stumbled out of the river and slowly made her way back to the warehouse.

Inside the warehouse, Jethro Barking rubbed his hands on his orange robe and stroked his sore head. He sneered down at the three children, as they lay trussed up on the floor, then gave a short derisive snort.

'I never thought you'd come back,' he growled, 'but you did, and I am so glad because it means you know the secret of the thorn hedge. You won't escape this time. When you've told me where the gate in the hedge is to be found, I'll be back in the real world and, before you know it, wealthy beyond belief.'

He walked over to Milly and poked her in the stomach with his foot. 'You pushed me into the river and that shark nearly caught me, but I escaped, and now you are going to tell me where the square branch is.' Milly choked and strained at her ropes but they were so firmly tied she couldn't move an inch.

Turning his attention to George, the former head of the orphanage crouched down, put his face close to George's and said in an angry hiss, 'Where is the square branch? Why are you here? Where are my diamonds!'

There was no reply; George had nothing to say.

'Diamonds...' said Jethro Barking, scratching at his chin. 'I'll bet you have come back for more diamonds! Well you won't get any, and maybe tomorrow, when the Mutton's teeth are about to tear you limb from limb, you'll tell me where the branch is.'

George still said nothing. Old Barking Mad roared with rage at the boy's stubborn silence.

'I'll peg you out one at a time until you talk! You can watch each other die, how about that?'

Worn out from the fight and all the shouting, Jethro eventually retired to his room, slamming the door as he went. For hours the prisoners could hear the big man pacing up and down muttering to himself. It was mostly incoherent rambling about how a mere slip of a girl could elude them all. He raged and threatened but neither Drago nor Singer were found.

A small light glowed in the centre of the room where a guard sat in a chair, staring at the captives lying trussed up on the floor. Behind the guard there was a table on which stood a large, heavy vase filled with flowers. Jangle liked to keep the room bright and cheerful and maintained a small garden at the back of the warehouse stocked with a variety of brightly coloured blooms. But Jangle was gone now; the Robes had untied him, cursed him for being a useless Minling, and taken him away to help look for Singer. George hoped he had managed to lead them far enough in the wrong direction.

It was the middle of the night, when the sleepy guard's head was beginning to nod, that the three children saw the bunch of flowers rise slowly into the air. They were all in great discomfort from the tight ropes binding them, so were wide awake. Watching with wide eyes and bated breath, they saw the flowers slide out of the vase and drift gently down to land on the table. Then the vase floated into the air and moved silently towards the guard. It rose high above him then swiftly descended squarely onto his head. There was a crunching noise and the guard toppled over and slid to the ground with a gentle thump.

Nobody moved or spoke as they listened for any indication that the noise had disturbed the sleeping Robes in the other room. To their relief nothing could be heard, then a quiet voice said, 'Be visible,' and with a shimmer in the soft light, Singer Smith appeared bending over the guard.

'He'll be all right,' she whispered and placed the vase back on the table, and returned the flowers. Moving over to Milly she started to undo the knotted rope that bound her.

'Singer, that was fantastic,' said George in a low voice.

'Well done, Singer,' added Charlie, his black eyes shining with excitement.

When she was free, Milly started on Charlie's knots while Singer turned her attention to George. Before long they were all free and whispering together in the middle of the room.

'Can I go and punch Old Barking Mad?' hissed Milly, wanting to use her powers to full effect.

'No you cannot,' said George. 'Thank goodness for Singer and her new power. We'd really be in trouble if she hadn't come with us. Well done Singer.' The others added further congratulations.

Singer smiled shyly. 'I didn't know what else to do,' she whispered.

'Did you see what happened to Drago?' asked Milly anxiously. The thought of him drowning in the river had worried her all night.

'He should be safe,' whispered Singer. 'I pushed a log into the river and he scrambled onto it and was drifting off to the other bank when I left him. Batty was with him and trying to help. She still had the king's crown in her claws and wouldn't let go of it.'

'Good old Batty!' exclaimed Charlie. 'Losing that crown seems to have driven Old Barking Mad even more insane.'

'Hush,' said Milly, as Charlie's voice got louder.

'What now?' asked Singer. 'Where do we go?'

They moved to the window and peeped out. There were enough glimmering lights outside to show the Robe's boat tied up on the quay and an orange-gowned guard sitting on deck with his head bowed as if half asleep. For a moment there was silence as they tried to work out a plan of action.

'We'll borrow the Robes' boat,' said George, 'then we can go through the Rainbow Cave in comfort. It's a big, fast boat, so we should get clean away. Jangle won't have to lend us his boat so he won't get the blame.'

'But what about him?' said Milly, pointing towards the door.

George shook his head. 'Old Barking Mad is

stuck here and we must make sure he can never get back through the hedge. He needs one of us to tell him where the square branch is so he can return, and that is something that must *never* happen. But right now, we need to get away. We can't risk him waking up.'

'There's a guard outside we need to deal with' said Milly, keen to see a bit more action. 'Shall I go and punch him?'

'No,' hissed George. 'We want to remove him quietly so he won't raise the alarm straight away. Singer will have to distract him somehow.' He looked at Singer. 'And I think I know how. Come with me.'

Quietly they tiptoed across the room as George whispered some instructions.

'Be invisible,' whispered Singer, once she had grasped the plan, and disappeared.

The door to the warehouse opened very slowly to let out the invisible Singer. It was left open just enough for George, Milly and Charlie to peep through and watch the guard.

The gangplank onto the boat bent slightly as it took Singer's weight. She had picked up a large stone and they could see it suspended in the air as she moved up the jetty.

The guard never stirred.

Suddenly, as if by magic, the stone was thrown into the air and landed in the water on the far side of the boat. There was a resounding splash and the guard's head jerked upright. He scrambled to his feet and hurried to the side of the boat to investigate.

George watched closely. The guard leaned over the edge to stare down into the water, then suddenly seemed to throw himself into the river. He only had time to reach out with his hands, as if to save himself, before he hit the surface and plunged into the depths. As he struggled towards the bank, the river carried him away from the warehouse.

George opened the door, rushed up the gangplank and onto the boat. He called urgently to the others to join him. Milly took some time to salvage the bags of provisions from Jangle's kitchen before rushing out to join George and Singer. Charlie hurried to untie the rope that kept the boat close to the quay. Once they were all on board, George started the engine.

The strange energy that powered the Robes' boat was quiet but powerful. George let the boat chug gently into the middle of the river. Behind them they saw the swimming Robe had made it to the bank. His cries grew fainter as the boat moved slowly upstream towards the Rainbow Cave.

5

THE NOGOODLANDS

'Wait for me!' came a cry. It was a squeaky voice and came from above them.

'Batty!' they all shouted at once.

With a flurry of tick-tocking, the bird landed clumsily on the deck. 'I hate flying at night,' she said, 'but I saw that Robe dive into the river and you lot running for the boat, and I thought, *They've escaped!* Then I thought, *Wherever they're going, I'm going too!* So here I am.'

'Where's Drago? Is he all right?' asked Singer.

'As far as I know. I left him sitting on the bank of the river with the king's crown perched on his head. He said he was going to seek shelter and lie low.'

'Good idea!' said George. 'He must be quite shaken by his ordeal in the water.'

'Did you see me attack the king? Wasn't I brilliant?' said Batty in an excited voice.

'You were amazing,' agreed Milly.

'When I get my crown back off Drago, I shall be Queen of the Tick-Tocks!'

Milly smiled, then said with a frown, 'I hope Drago will safe. Do you think we should go back for him?'

Batty shook her head.

'He said to go on. He knows a place where he can hide.'

Milly sighed. 'How will we manage without him?'

The river meandered slowly up towards the cliffs and the boat chugged along against the current. All conversation stopped as the cliffs towered above them and the black hole that was the tunnel leading to the cave became bigger. Choppy water lapped against the sides of the boat as the river flowed faster out of the tunnel. To avoid the splashes, the children sat together in the middle of the boat, apart from Charlie, who sat at the very front, staring eagerly ahead.

'I know creatures can't be changed twice,' said Batty, 'but I don't like the Rainbow Cave, so I am now going to hide. Let me know when we reach the other side.' She fluttered off the bench and into the cabin.

George called out to Charlie. 'And you Charlie, it's dangerous to sit out on the deck; you could get changed and you might not like it.'

There was no reply.

The light rapidly disappeared as they entered the tunnel and the boat frequently bumped into the walls as it sailed into total blackness.

'Go on, Charlie,' called George. 'Get inside the cabin!'

'I want to get changed,' came the defiant reply. 'I don't care how; I'm staying here.' The boy hunched up in his seat and gripped the side of the boat. 'I wouldn't miss this for the world,' he added and sounded very determined.

George shook his head in exasperation, but there was nothing he could do about it.

Very soon, flashing lights ahead indicated the Rainbow Cave was looming. A roll of thunder suddenly echoed round the cave and the noise vibrated in the tunnel all around them. When the boat reached the cave a bright light shone from high above. Looking up, they saw a blanket of white mist that stretched like an endless ceiling in every direction.

A short while later a humming noise started and grew steadily louder. The light slowly changed to a deep red that bathed everything around them.

Gazing in wonder, the children's faces glowed red too.

The red changed to orange, then to yellow then green. The children felt a chill come over them as the green changed to blue and pulled their collars and shawls tighter.

Another deep rumble of thunder overhead followed the flashing of bright, white lightning that sizzled and crackled all around them, bouncing off the walls of the cave in a flurry of hectic sparks.

Everyone put their hands over their ears and shut their eyes. They yelled and shouted with fright at the deafening noise and blinding light. It was only when the colour of the light changed to violet that the noise subsided and silence enveloped them once more. Cautiously, they sat up and looked around to find they were still in the middle of the lake. A violet mist hung overhead, pulling the last few remaining flashes and sparks up into itself, while more patches of mist hovered over the water.

Soon they were lit once again by the dim white light they had started with and the water in the lake appeared calm as it lapped gently against the hull of their boat.

'That was fantastic!' yelled Charlie, leaping to his feet with excitement. 'I'll bet I've been changed; I'm going to be the best fighter in the world.'

Milly looked worried. 'I do hope you haven't been changed; I like you as you are. But if you have, I hope it'll be something useful.'

Bits of seaweed passing by showed which way

the river was flowing and the direction they must steer the boat. Scrambling towards the bow, Charlie called out, 'I see a light ahead!'

The bright circle of light showed them the exit and George headed straight for it.

Full of excitement at what his new found power might be, Charlie jumped up and down on top of the cabin as the boat emerged from the Rainbow Cave. He flexed the muscles in his arms and looked for a heavy weight to lift.

'That was awesome!' he cried. 'The lights, the thunder, the lightning, I tingled all over. I must have been changed in some way.'

'I didn't find out about my power for months after I went through the Rainbow Cave,' said Singer.

'I found out that I could talk straight away,' said Batty as she emerged from the cabin and perched on George's head. She cackled loudly with laughter as she remembered Jangle's surprise when she first spoke to him.

'I'm no stronger than I was before,' said Charlie as he tried to lift a box from the deck. His voice was bitter with disappointment. Then a thought occurred to him.

'Maybe I have to get angry before I get strong,' he said, looking a little more hopeful. 'Stamp on my toe Milly. Make me angry!'

'I will not!' she said.

'Then call me names or something,' Charlie sounded desperate.

'No, I won't do that either,' said Milly.

Charlie turned to Singer and looked at her hopefully.

'I won't either,' said the girl.

'I will,' said Batty in her squeaky voice, and the bird flew off her perch and hovered over Charlie. 'You are a despicable little garbage pot, with cauliflower ears, a squashed tomato nose and a head like a fried pumpkin.'

Batty was getting warmed up. 'You have a brain the size of a wizened prune and you are so ugly that even the crocodiles all round this boat wouldn't eat you.'

'Maybe I can swim like George,' said Charlie and taking off his shirt moved to the side of the boat.

'Those crocodiles will probably spit you out,' shrieked Batty and she cackled again.

Charlie obviously wasn't listening to the bird and didn't realise that the floating logs around the boat were actually crocodiles. He was about to dive when Milly shrieked, 'Don't jump!'

In anticipation of its next meal, one of the crocodiles Charlie had thought was only a floating log opened its mouth wide. Charlie looked down, screamed with shock and leapt away from the side.

Concern for Charlie's nonexistent power was forgotten as the children crowded to the side of the boat to look at the crocodiles. The deceptive looking creatures were floating towards them from all over the river.

'Full speed ahead George,' called out Milly.

'Let's get away from these brutes.'

The river was wide and slow moving and George was able to steer slowly around the big creatures. When he saw a gap, he accelerated and managed to get clear of the crocodiles. It was a quick boat and it wasn't long before they were travelling along without being followed.

Most of the day was spent cruising up the river. From time to time other boats came floating down in the opposite direction. The occupants always stood up and saluted them by extending a clenched fist high in the air. At first, Milly and Singer would also stand up and gracefully acknowledge the salutation.

'I'm not sure that's a good idea,' said George. 'They obviously recognise this boat and expect to see the King of the Robes on board. It might prove very awkward when they realise we have stolen it, particularly when we come back. You realise that Old Barking Mad will stop at nothing to capture at least one of us.'

Charlie searched in the cabin and found an orange gown. He draped it over his shoulders and came on deck in time to acknowledge the salutes from some Robes on another passing boat. It was doubtful that anyone was fooled by the tiny figure of Charlie pretending to be the King of the Robes, but it confused some of them long enough for the boat to pass without incident.

A great curve in the river took them through more

open countryside and the City of the Robes came gradually into view. The Dome that housed the mysterious energy plant loomed large in front of them and it was here that the river split into two.

Charlie pointed towards the part of the river that led to the right and up towards some hills in the distance. 'That's where the Waterlanders came from!' he said.

George turned the boat in that direction and soon a dense forest crowded in on them, replacing the meadows and open spaces they were used to. They sat quietly and listened to the strange noises coming from the forest. There were distant roars that sounded like lions and a lot of gibbering, squeaky chatter from monkey-like creatures that jumped from the branches of the passing trees. Above them birds flew high in the sky and once a large hawk hovered over them as if scanning the boat for a likely meal. It was all very intimidating and the friends bunched together in the middle of the boat for comfort. Batty was by far the most afraid and she trembled in Milly's arms, cowering out of sight of the great bird.

The river gradually widened into a small lake with several tributaries running into it on either side. At the far end, cliffs surrounding a high plateau ran to their lowest point where a waterfall cascaded down creating choppy waves that circled out into the centre of the lake. After sailing around the lake they came to a stop in the middle of it.

'Which way do we go?' asked George thoroughly confused by all the choices. 'There are three rivers feeding this lake, all wide enough for this boat. Which one do we take?'

'Batty could fly high and see which river comes from the hills!' suggested Singer.

They all looked at Batty expectantly.

'Are you all stark raving mad,' said the bird. 'How long do you think a noisy Tick-Tock would last up there? You saw that beastly looking hawk, do you want him to dine on a rather plump bird that talks too much,' Batty was quite indignant.

'Sorry, Batty,' said George. 'Of course you must stay here.'

'We should land and climb a tree,' said Charlie. 'I can do it, I might not be as fast as Sam but I can climb just as high. In fact I might have a power that makes me run and climb just like Sam.'

It seemed the only option so George steered the boat to a dry part of the bank and Charlie jumped ashore.

'Don't go too far,' called Singer anxiously, 'you could easily get lost in the forest.'

'I'll go with him,' said Milly suddenly and jumped onto the bank. 'He might need my help.'

'We'll explore around the lake again,' George shouted after them. 'Call out to us when you are ready. It's probably safer to be in a boat than in the forest.'

Charlie and Milly walked along a path where the forest was less dense, but no suitable trees could be found. To make sure they didn't get lost, Milly kept plucking yellow flowers that grew in the undergrowth and laying them on the ground as they went.

Charlie started running to see if he had a power, but he wasn't any faster than normal. He stopped and frowned. Then he called out, 'Be invisible,' but nothing happened. 'I must have some sort of power,' he muttered, as he continued walking along.

'Don't worry, Charlie,' said Milly, placing a reassuring hand on his shoulder. 'You'll find your gift when you need it.'

'I want it now,' he snorted.

'When you *need* it,' Milly repeated, and for a while the pair of them walked on in silence.

Ahead of them the path slowly widened into an

expanse of open meadow. Charlie stopped and stood still, a confused look on his face.

'What's the matter?' asked Milly.

'I can hear voices, there's somebody here!' he whirled round and stared at the trees and the undergrowth.

Milly looked around as well. 'I heard an animal grunting somewhere, but I didn't hear voices,' she said.

Charlie looked puzzled.

'Somebody said, *Where have these strange creatures come from?* It's talking about us.'

'If you can hear me, please raise your arms,' commanded a voice from nowhere.

Charlie nervously raised his arms and said, 'We come in peace.'

Milly turned and looked at her friend with a deep frown.

'What did you say?' she asked.

'I said, *We come in peace.* Why?'

'You're talking in funny grunts. I couldn't understand you,' said Milly in alarm. 'And why are you holding your hands up?'

'Someone told me to raise my arms and so I said, *We come in peace.* It seemed like a sensible thing to say.'

Milly shrugged. 'It just sounded like grunts to me, as if you were speaking their language...'

Charlie stared at Milly in amazement. 'What's happening?'

'I think you may have found your gift!' she said.

'Say something else.'

Charlie glanced around again, looking for a creature to talk to. 'We mean you no harm,' he said. 'Show yourself.'

Again, Milly heard him speak in strange grunts.

'Right in front of you,' came the voice that only Charlie could understand.

In the middle of the path was a large shrub with broad, purple leaves. Charlie realised that the voice came from somewhere in amongst those leaves. Cautiously, he approached the shrub.

It was a little bit taller than he was and quite wide. Small, yellow fruits dangled from the thorny branches. As he reached out to part the leaves, the thorns suddenly retracted and the branches became smooth. Charlie froze in surprise and then cautiously leant forward and peeped inside. In the centre of the shrub there was a protrusion like a rugby ball on top of a thick tree trunk. On the top of it were two small lumps. As Charlie examined it, the lumps opened up and two huge eyes stared back at him. He leapt backwards and stumbled to the ground. The rugby ball grunted, sounding like a very distant rumble of thunder. Charlie realised that the rugby ball was actually a head.

'Come on in and say hello,' invited the rugby ball.

Cautiously, Charlie parted the leaves once more and saw a sideways slit in the bottom of the ball, with the corners turned up in the shape of a smile, albeit a rather crooked one. The two eyes stared at him, blinked, then looked at the ground. Looking down, Charlie saw there was plenty of room around the base of the trunk for him to sit, so he settled himself into the space and crossed his legs.

Milly's anxious voice came from the path. 'Charlie, be careful.'

'It's all right,' he called back. 'I think it's friendly.'

The eyes blinked at him again and the smile rearranged itself into another form of crookedness, though managed to be no less welcoming for all that.

'You are the only creature I have ever come across who can speak the Polly tree language,' the ball said at last. 'You must be very clever.'

'Just gifted,' Charlie answered with a smirk. 'Who are you?'

Outside the shrub, Milly listened, but all she could hear were strange grunts and odd snarls.

'I am a Polly tree.'

'A what?' asked Charlie.

'A Polly tree.'

Charlie scratched his head. 'I've never heard of a Polly tree.'

'There are a lot of us around,' the tree made the distant rumbling noise again and Charlie realised it was chuckling.

'I'm Charlie,' he said, wondering where to offer his hand. 'And the girl standing out there with her mouth wide open is Milly.'

'Pleased to meet you,' said the Polly tree politely, and gently stroked one of its leaves against the offered hand. 'May I ask what are you doing here?'

'We're sailing up the river looking for the Waterlanders,' grunted Charlie and, hoping the Polly tree would be able to help, he added, 'We're a bit lost, actually.'

'I'd like to help you,' said the tree, 'but although we Polly trees can move about, it's a bit of a nuisance pulling up roots and wobbling around until you find somewhere to wriggle them back into the ground and all that...'

Charlie nodded, looking at the tangled mass of roots at the creatures base.

'I can imagine...'

'So I'm afraid,' the tree continued, 'I have no idea where the Waterlanders come from. Sometimes I see them wander past me, but as they are frightened of the Snakeheads, they don't stick around for long.'

'Who are the Snakeheads?' asked Charlie.

'Oh dear, you are a complete stranger to these lands, I fear. The Snakeheads live in the swamps and usually kill and eat any creature they can catch. Everyone here avoids them but they are cunning and often catch Jambucks and even, from time to time, horses.'

'Horses!' gasped Charlie.

'Screech grunt!' heard Milly.

'It has been known,' continued the Polly tree.

'Mind you the Jambucks will know where the Waterlanders live and you, with your strange ability, might even be able to talk to them. Very few can understand what they say.'

'Where do we find the Jambucks?'

'Find the horses,' grunted the Polly tree, 'they all live near each other. When the Snakeheads come hunting, the Jambucks leap on the horses and they all gallop away. Jambucks can only run slowly; the Snakeheads would always catch them if they didn't have the horses to help.'

'Don't the horses mind?' asked Charlie.

'No, the Jambucks help the horses too, you see. They have fingers you know, just like you. Very useful fingers are, and they do all sorts of things for the horses.'

'Well fancy that!' said Charlie, then called out to Milly. 'Can you see any horses out there?'

Milly moved past the Polly tree and gazed out into the meadow beyond. 'Yes,' she called back, 'and lots of bouncy things like little kangaroos.'

'Those will be the Jambucks,' said the Polly tree. 'You'd better go; the Snakeheads use this path and you really do need to avoid them. Pop in on your way back and we'll have another chat.'

'Don't the Snakeheads bother you?' asked Charlie, standing to leave.

'After all the years we've been here, the Snakeheads still don't know what we are. They may be cunning, but they're not very bright.' The Polly tree gave a deep, gurgling laugh. 'They never even notice when we move, and they don't like the thorns, so they just dismiss us as normal trees. They do try to take my fruit, but I can move my thorns around so they get scratched and have to go away.'

'We won't take your fruit then,' said Charlie,

looking at the little yellow globes that hung off the branches.

'Oh you must take some with you,' said Polly. 'But don't eat any unless you want to fall asleep straight away. The Snakeheads use them to make their victims fall asleep. They dig pits and trap Jambucks and other animals, then throw them food, mixed with my fruits. Then...' said the Polly tree sadly, 'they cook them and eat them. That's why I try very hard not to let Snakeheads pick my fruit!'

Charlie plucked one of the fruits. It felt smooth but firm in his hand, so he tucked it into his trouser pocket. With another brush of hand against leaf, Charlie thanked the Polly tree, promised to come and see him again, then stepped back onto the path to rejoin Milly.

'Where are we going now,' she asked as they headed up the path towards the meadow.

'To talk to the horses,' he replied, taking her hand in his. 'Come on.'

Looking anxiously all around, Milly and Charlie walked towards the meadow. Charlie told her everything the Polly tree had said and so they decided they would try to make contact with the Jambucks before climbing a tree to see which way the rivers went.

Milling around in the meadow were lots of small horses. Mixed in among them, also eating the grass, were the small bouncing creatures that the Polly tree had called Jambucks. They waved at the horses, but were afraid to call out in case the Snakeheads heard them.

Unfortunately, there was little response from the horses or the Jambucks, so they started to walk nervously out into the meadow and towards them.

'I'd rather be a fighter than a translator,' grumbled Charlie.

'Nonsense,' said Milly. 'It's useful that we all have different powers, and yours will be invaluable, I'm sure.'

Charlie was about to say something else, but before he could speak, the ground beneath them collapsed. With a cry of alarm, they tumbled together into a deep pit, landing in a crumpled heap. With stunned groans, they untangled themselves and checked for injury. Apart from a small bruise on Milly's forehead and a few minor scratches, there seemed to be no real damage done.

On looking around however, they found the pit to be too deep, and the walls too smooth, for them to climb out, even with Milly standing on Charlie's shoulders.

'The Snakeheads,' said Milly. 'The Polly tree warned us, and we still fell into the trap.'

Charlie pointed to a bowl in the corner of the pit that contained what looked like chopped fruit salad.

'Look, he said, 'Polly tree fruit. We're supposed to eat it and fall asleep.'

'We have to get out of here,' said Milly in a panic. 'HELP!' she shouted at the top of her voice. 'HELP!'

'Hush!' said Charlie. 'The Snakeheads will hear

you!'

'They're coming anyway; what else can we do?' Charlie shrugged.

'I don't know... I'm sure I'll think of something...'

6

SNAKEHEADS

Shouting for help seemed to be useless so they started trying to dig footholds in the side of the pit. Sadly, all they got were very dirty hands and sore fingers. Whilst they were struggling, two heads appeared over the edge and stared down at them. One head belonged to a small horse and looked at them with curiosity. 'Who are you?' it asked.

'Milly and Charlie,' replied Charlie, holding his hands out in despair, 'but we haven't got time to chat. Please get us out of here!'

'How?' asked the horse, then, turning to the creature alongside it, said, 'Can you help?'

The second head belonged to a strange looking creature. It had bright black eyes, big floppy ears, and a face shaped like a dog. The creature raised a small hand and scratched an ear thoughtfully.

Although it didn't actually speak, it did emit a high pitched whistle which Charlie found he could make sense of. 'These poor creatures have no hope,' it said to the horse. 'The Snakeheads will be here soon and I haven't got time to go for a rope.'

Charlie whistled back.

'I can hear you. I can speak with you. Please help us!'

The Jambuck, for this is what the strange creature was, jumped back startled. He then leaned over the edge of the pit to study the two trapped children a little more closely. Charlie continued to whistle.

'If Milly stands on my back, maybe she can reach your hand. Then at least she can escape. Believe me, when the Snakeheads arrive, she won't be taken prisoner very easily.'

The Jambuck crooked its head slightly.

'You can talk to me,' it said, sounding surprised. 'Apart from the horses, very few can understand Jambuck talk. Who are you?'

'Visitors from a long way away. Can you try to reach us?'

The Jambuck scratched its head and looked up at the sky, apparently lost in thought. Then it looked down into the pit again, nodded and reached out a hand.

Turning to Milly, Charlie explained what had happened. 'I can talk to the Jambuck. He's going to help us. Stand on my shoulders and see if he can pull you up.'

Charlie leaned against the wall of the pit; Milly put one foot into his cupped hands and he lifted her onto his shoulders. The Jambuck reached down as much as he could. His hand was only a few inches away from Milly's.

'I'm going to jump for it,' cried Milly. Immediately she bent her knees and leapt upwards to catch hold of the Jambuck's hand.

It worked! The small hand grasped Milly's wrist

firmly, and for a moment she was suspended in the air. The Jambuck took a deep breath, heaved upwards, and Milly clambered her way up towards the top of the pit. Just as Charlie thought the Jambuck would pull her clear, the edge of the pit crumbled and the Jambuck slithered over the edge. Bravely, it held onto Milly's arm, but although its back legs scrabbled for a hold, it was no use. The Jambuck and Milly tumbled down into the pit and landed in a heap at Charlie's feet.

Charlie bent over the Jambuck to see if it was hurt. It really did look a lot like a small kangaroo. It had strong back legs and a thick tail, and was covered in reddish-brown fur. He stroked it gently, but the creature did not move.

'I think it banged its head,' he said to Milly, who was picking herself up and dusting off her dress.

She was about to speak when they heard a great commotion from up above. Looking up, she and Charlie saw the horse stamping at the ground with evident distress.

'The Snakeheads are coming!' it cried. 'I'm sorry. I'm so sorry.' With a final, sad look, the horse turned tail and ran.

Milly and Charlie looked at each other.

'Now what do we do?' Milly asked. Charlie shrugged.

The sound of several pairs of stamping, scuffling feet announced the imminent arrival of the Snakeheads.

'Hide the Polly fruit!' hissed Milly. 'Then pretend

to be asleep. They'll think we've eaten it and pull us out. We may be able to escape later.'

'I hope you're right,' said Charlie, as he began to bury the fruits under the loose soil. Then he lay down next to Milly and pretended to be asleep.

Eyes tight shut, they could hear sniffing sounds and some appreciative muttering. They sensed the Snakeheads were peering over the edge of the pit and looking down at them.

'Good, good... Two strange creatures and a Jambuck.' The voice they heard was more of a sustained hiss than anything like speech. 'A very fine catch!'

'I can understand what they are saying,' Charlie whispered to Milly.

'Don't speak to them yet,' murmured Milly. 'Pretend you're unconscious.'

Charlie opened his eyes a crack to see a ladder sliding down the side of the pit. Seconds later a Snakehead stood in front of him, examining its prey.

It was a large creature with a yellow and black scaly body and thick, strong arms. When it leaned over to peer at him, Charlie saw a snakelike head with slit eyes and a tongue which flickered in and out of a mouth full of sharp, little teeth. Charlie snapped his eyes shut and his body started to quiver with fright.

The next instant, those same strong arms lifted him into the air like a sack of straw. He was carried up the ladder and dropped roughly onto the ground at the top of the pit. Moments later there was a thump as Milly's body joined him, then a smaller thump as the Jambuck landed next to them. Next, the three captives were dumped into the back of a cart pulled by a slave horse.

'These two are very special,' Charlie heard the voice of a Snakehead hiss nearby. 'We've never caught such tasty looking creatures before.'

He felt rough ropes being pulled tight around his wrists and ankles. With a sudden jolt, the cart began to move.

As they lay in the back of the cart, jerking from side to side as it wound its way along the dirt track, they heard a familiar tick-tocking sound high above them. Moments later, the voice of Batty could be heard, berating the hideous beasts.

'You won't get away with this you nasty, slit-eyed monsters! I'll get help, and you'll pay dearly for hurting my friends.'

Although they didn't understand what the bird was saying, the Snakeheads hissed and screeched at the bothersome creature above them.

Batty was unimpressed. 'I'll bring all sorts of help and you'll be sorry, you'll see!' she shrieked defiantly, then flapped higher into the air and was gone.

The cart rumbled along until it arrived at the Snakeheads' village. When it stopped moving, a number of the Snakeheads peered into the back to see what bounty had been brought home. Charlie and Milly found the sudden appearance of a row of leering heads staring at them extremely unnerving.

They snapped their eyes shut immediately and lay as still as they could while scaly hands dragged them out of the cart. The hands felt slimy and cold and the children quivered with revulsion and fear.

Once more Milly risked opening her eyes a fraction and saw a circle of huts made out of wood and straw. In front of the huts there was a great iron cauldron resting on a metal grill. Black and yellow Snakeheads of all shapes and sizes were everywhere. As the captives were carried towards the giant pot, heads turned to stare at them. The hissing and spitting was bad enough, but the glimpses they got of long, thin tongues flicking out of narrow mouths in anticipation of a tasty meal to come, was almost too much to bear. Milly wanted to tear at her bindings, but didn't dare risk the Snakeheads finding out she was awake. Finally, they were dumped into the great iron pot, one after the other.

'Did you hear Batty?' whispered Milly when she felt sure the Snakeheads had left them alone.

'I certainly did,' replied Charlie, and he gave a little smile at the angry way Batty had shouted at the Snakeheads.

'I'm sorry I couldn't pull you out,' the Jambuck whistled.

Turning to look at the little creature, he saw that it had recovered consciousness and he replied, 'Thanks for trying. Are you all right now?'

'I just have a small headache, but it is of little consequence. By the time it clears up, I'll be dead.'

'I'm so sorry we got you into this mess. What is

your name?' asked Charlie.

'Tatu,' came the reply. 'But we haven't much time together, we are about to be cooked.'

'What!' Charlie's shocked whistle filled Milly with alarm.

'What are you talking about?' she interrupted.

'His name is Tatu and he says we are about to be cooked.

Milly gasped. 'I hope he's wrong.'

They both struggled and twisted and finally managed to stand upright and peer over the edge of the great pot. Walking towards them were three Snakeheads carrying a pile of chopped wood in their short stubby arms. When they looked down they saw that the pot was standing on a metal grill and, under that, a pile of wood was already in place.

'Speak to them, Charlie,' urged Milly. 'Tell them we are too young and thin to be cooked.'

The Snakeheads threw their load of wood into the pit underneath the cauldron. As they turned to go, Charlie hissed at them. 'I speak your language, you can't cook us, we are not food!' he said.

The Snakeheads looked at him in surprise and came closer to stare at him. Abruptly Charlie sat down in the bottom of the cauldron.

The heads that peered over the edge of the cauldron to hiss at the frightened children were attached to thick necks which twisted downwards to look at Charlie.

'This tasty morsel speaks like one of us,' hissed one. Then it looked at Tatu and Milly. 'Can you speak to these pieces of food as well?' it added.

'Of cause I can. I can speak to any creature in any language,' Charlie boasted.

The heads disappeared and they could hear them talking amongst themselves. Charlie listened intently. 'They're amazed I can speak to them. I think they're going to take us out,' he said to Milly and Tatu.

Sure enough, a Snakehead leaned into the pot and, grabbing Charlie, lifted him out.

Charlie was dragged away. 'What about my friends?' he shouted in the Snakeheads language.

'We will eat them soon,' replied the reptile as he held onto Charlie's arm and pulled him along towards the huts. 'But you may be useful. We'll keep you for a little while longer...'

Back in the cauldron, Milly struggled to her feet. Peering over the edge, she looked for Charlie. He was standing by the biggest hut surrounded by Snakeheads. When they moved away, she saw that he had been fitted with an iron collar attached to a long chain. More Snakeheads came towards her carrying buckets full of water which they tipped into the pot. She slipped and fell onto her back.

The Jambuck looked at her with sad brown eyes which seemed to say, 'I told you so, we are going to be cooked.' Milly wanted to talk to him, but without Charlie to translate, it was useless.

Slowly the cauldron was filled with water and she had to stand up to avoid being drowned.

Unfortunately, Tatu, who only came up to her waist, was having greater difficulty keeping his head up. With her hands tied behind her back, Milly couldn't lift him, so she leaned forwards and let him put his arms around her neck. When she stood up straight, the Jambuck came up with her and hung on tight.

The water had reached up to her chest when she heard a voice she knew well. It came from outside the pot and it belonged to Singer Smith. 'I'm coming in with you, watch out.'

Singer was invisible, but Milly heard her climb into the pot, then there was a sudden splash and she was standing next to her, curiously outlined by the water.

'We got worried when you didn't return, so Batty and I volunteered to go and find you,' she whispered.

'Thank goodness you did, those monsters were going to eat us,' Milly still couldn't believe it.

'I'm going to untie your ropes now,' said Singer.

Singer took a deep breath and ducking down, untied the knots around Milly's feet and hands. Then the startled Jambuck had his ropes undone by a creature he couldn't see, save for a shimmer in the water.

'I'm ready for them now,' Milly said to Singer. 'Let me out of this pot and I'll show them how to fight.'

'No,' said Singer urgently. 'There are too many of them. We'll have to run for it. Batty will show us the way; she's up there somewhere trying to be quiet.'

'We can't leave Charlie!' cried Milly frantically.

'He knows I'm here, but I can't help him yet; there are Snakeheads all around him. He says you must escape first. I'll come back when it's dark and set him free, but for now we have to get you out of here before they turn you into stew.'

Reluctantly, Milly agreed. With a heave, she lifted Tatu out of the cauldron. The Jambuck clung to the edge of it for a moment before dropping to the ground. Milly followed and clambered out to join her new friend.

'Be visible!' the voice of Singer was no longer a whisper.

Tatu jumped in surprise when Singer appeared right in front of him and turned a bewildered face to Milly.

'Don't worry, Tatu,' Milly reassured him. 'This is Singer. Sometimes she's invisible and sometimes she's not. You can come with us if you like, but we must run. Now!'

Tatu simply looked puzzled for a moment.

'Follow me!' said Singer.

The Jambuck didn't know what had been said, but he wasn't about to be left behind.

Just then, they were spotted by a nearby Snakehead who immediately let out a great roar and started to chase after them. Singer took off, running as fast as she could along the edge of the forest. Milly was right behind her and, with a two legged hop, the Jambuck followed them.

'This way!' The familiar screech of an excited

Batty came from above. The Tick-Tock bird had fluttered overhead and, now they had escaped, she swooped down to give them encouragement. 'Run Milly,' she cried. 'Show those silly newts who can run the fastest!'

A quick glance behind surprised Milly; more Snakeheads had joined the chase and they were running much faster than she had expected. In spite of Batty's encouragement, the Snakeheads would soon be upon them. It looked as though she would have to turn and fight before they reached the safety of the boat on the lake.

A short distance ahead they saw the path that led through the forest. As the Snakeheads gained ground, they whooped with delight. The leaders of the pack were closing in on the Jambuck, who was struggling to keep up with the girls. Singer stopped as she reached the path and so did Milly.

'Disappear,' ordered Milly to Singer as she grabbed the hand of Tatu and pulled him along the path into the forest. The Jambuck was gasping for breath and looked exhausted. Milly realised that pulling him along was hopeless; Tatu's hopping made her arm bounce up and down and all she did was make him fall over. If she left him, he was sure to be taken, but if she stayed, she could not be certain of being able to fight all the Snakeheads at once and defend Tatu at the same time.

'Oh, Charlie...' she cried, as if he were with her. 'What shall I do?'

Then she saw the tree.

Was it the same Polly tree they had seen earlier? She couldn't be sure, but she did remember how Charlie had disappeared inside its branches. Now it could be their only hope.

'Help us Polly tree, please!' she cried. Whether the tree would understand her or not, she couldn't possibly know, but as soon as she spoke, the branches opened wide. It was offering them a hiding place.

Without hesitation, Milly dragged Tatu into the tree and snuggled up around its trunk. The dense branches and leaves closed around them and they stayed very still, too frightened to move.

Outside the Polly tree they heard Singer scream with shock at the way the tree had swallowed them up.

'Don't worry, Singer, the tree is a friend. We're safe here,' she called out. 'Just stay invisible and keep out of the way.'

'I'll lead them away from you,' Singer replied, and within seconds they heard her calling to the Snakeheads.

'Over here! Over here! This way!'

The Snakeheads skidded to a halt on the gravel, hissing and spitting in confusion. Then one of them shouted something and they all headed off in the direction of Singer's voice, away from the tree and its cowering occupants.

Milly and Tatu only started to relax when the noise of the chasing Snakeheads got fainter and finally disappeared. Milly wished that Charlie was with them and could speak to the Polly tree and thank it for saving them; all she could do was to stroke its leaves, say thank you, and hope it understood. With a loud rustle the branches opened up and Milly and Tatu crawled out from their hiding place.

Taking the Jambuck's hand, Milly started to walk down the path hoping they would be able to hide again if they heard the Snakeheads return. But Tatu had other ideas. The Jambuck pulled hard at Milly's hand, indicating that it wanted both of them to return to the meadowland rather than follow the Snakeheads and Singer into the forest.

Tatu seemed so determined that Milly let him pull her back along the path. When they reached the open space where the meadowlands stretched out as far as the eye could see, the Jambuck bounced up and down, getting higher and higher with each leap. After a while, he seemed satisfied and, with a smile, indicated that they should rest for a while.

Looking for a place to sit, they were startled by a noise behind them and whirled round just in time to see Singer reappear. Her pale face was smiling with relief at finding them safe, though she looked exhausted. The white dress she wore was spattered with dirt and torn in several places.

'What on earth was that tree doing?' she asked, panting heavily after her dash through the forest.

Milly told her about the Polly trees and Singer shook her head in amazement.

Tatu pulled on Milly's hand again and pointed across the meadow. About twenty small horses were galloping towards them. Riding on their backs were more of the Jambucks. Moments later they were surrounded by snorting horses all talking at once.

'Well done Tatu!' exclaimed a white horse and its rider, a Jambuck with extra large ears and a face wreathed in a smile, jumped to the ground and embraced Tatu.

The white horse looked at Milly. It was the same one that had peered at them when they had fallen into the pit. 'Not many creatures escape from the Snakeheads,' it commented. 'How did you manage it?'

Once again Milly marvelled at the way the horses spoke so easily to them and, although the answer was a bit complicated, she simply gestured to Singer and said, 'We had a little unseen help.' Singer Smith smiled at the white horse, who replied with a low nod of the head.

'We must not stay any longer,' said another horse. 'When the Snakeheads return, we need to be far away from here.'

'Do you know where the Waterlanders live?' Milly suddenly remembered that they were on a mission, and hoped the Jambucks would help them to their destination.

Her question was directed at Tatu, but it was the white horse who answered. 'They live in a land high above the great water slide, but only Waterlanders know how to climb the mountain. But you are very clever people with hands and feet like the Waterlanders, so perhaps the way will be shown to you.'

'We can't go without Charlie,' said Singer.

'Of course not,' agreed Milly. 'Let's get back to George and the boat and later, when it gets properly dark, we'll return and rescue Charlie.'

'Hush,' said Singer suddenly. 'I can hear the Snakeheads coming back.

The white horse snorted. 'We must go immediately,' he said, looking up in alarm.

The Jambucks leapt onto the backs of the horses and, with Batty safely tucked under one arm, Milly did the same. Singer followed suit and soon all the horses were racing across the meadow at breakneck speed. From a safe distance they turned and watched a dejected bunch of Snakeheads leave the forest and set off to return to their village.

'We can take you on a safer path to the lake,' said the white horse.

'Wait,' said Milly, and lifting Batty up, she spoke to the bird. 'Batty, we need to know that Charlie is still all right. Can you fly over the Snakeheads' camp and see where he is?'

Batty looked up at the sky.

'It's getting dark...' she said, a trace of nervousness in her voice.

'Then you'd better hurry,' said Milly, and flung the hesitant bird up into the air.

Flying over the treetops, her wings tick-tocking away, Batty saw a long procession of Snakeheads crossing the meadow. In the middle of the line, surrounded by the biggest, toughest looking Snakeheads, she saw two figures with ropes around their necks being dragged along. She was sure the smaller one was Charlie Trinder. As to whom the other figure was, she had no idea at all.

'We must get back to the boat quickly and get George,' Milly said after listening to Batty's report. 'The Snakeheads are taking Charlie away. We might lose him forever.'

'Why don't I go and help him now? They won't see me,' asked Singer, eager to save her friend as soon as possible.

'You won't get through,' said Batty. 'They got wise; he has some big guards around him, like a brick wall...'

'We will watch the Snakeheads from a distance,' said the white horse, 'and when you return, we can help you rescue your friend. The Jambucks will also help in any way they can. They are not strong, but they can be clever from time to time' he looked at Tatu as he spoke. By way of reply, Tatu made a few whistling noises and scratched at one of his floppy ears.

'Come with us now,' said a horse with a long black mane. 'We know a quick way to the lake.'

As the party moved off, Batty perched on Milly's shoulder. But as the horses began to speed up, she lost her balance and was forced to fly instead. Soon the horses turned onto a wide path which led down to the lakeside. A small wooden jetty jutted out into the water, right next to a deafening waterfall that cascaded down from the mountainside. George's boat was heading straight for the waterfall and immediately Milly and Singer waved to him.

Their relief at finding George turned to horror when they saw a flotilla of boats spread out behind him and forcing him to sail ever closer to the pounding waters of the waterfall. The pursuing boats were manned by orange gowned Robes who waved and cheered as they cut off every move George made to avoid capture.

Milly, Singer and the Jambucks gathered at the water's edge and the Robes spotted them. The boat that turned towards the jetty had a large Robe in the middle of it who roared louder than the rest. It was Jethro Barking and he was near enough to send a shiver down Singer's spine. His red, blotchy face was contorted with delight as he realised that he might be able to capture all the children who knew the secret of the hedge.

'We cannot help you anymore,' said the white horse. 'The forest down by the lakeside is too dense; we need open spaces to carry you.'

Tatu hopped down from his horse and pulled at Milly's arm.

'Go with Tatu,' said the white horse. 'He knows a way round the great white water slide.'

Anxiously, Milly and Singer dismounted and stared at the Robes' boat which had now stopped chasing George and was heading directly for the jetty. He was going to reach the jetty soon and it looked as though the other boats would force George into the pounding waterfall.

Tatu and the horses stared at each other as if deep in thought, then abruptly the horses wheeled around and clattered back down the path and away from the lake. Tatu darted into the forest, turning to check Milly and Singer were following him. Once again Milly was carrying Batty under one arm as she struggled through the undergrowth after Tatu. All of them were a lot smaller than the burly Robes. When Tatu made them squeeze through a narrow space between two giant rocks, Singer realised the Robes would never be able to follow them through the gap and she felt a lot safer.

Water started to spray all over them as Tatu led them along a tiny path towards the waterfall. The noise of the crashing water got louder then suddenly Tatu came to a dead end. A sheer rock face loomed across their path. To one side of the cliff, stood a large bush with prickly branches protecting bunches of small yellow fruit. Milly recognised them as the fruit of a Polly tree. Tatu stood in front of the tree and gave a series of looping whistles.

With a wide smile on his whiskery face, Tatu turned to face them just as the Polly tree pulled in its widespread branches. With a creak and a groan it leaned over to reveal a narrow slit in the rock. It had been protecting the entrance to a cave. Tatu darted through it and the two girls followed. Very quickly the narrow passageway opened up into a larger cave, which was hidden from the outside by the thick curtain of rushing water. Peering through the curtain, they could just see George's boat getting ever closer on the other side.

'We can save George!' declared Milly suddenly. 'We must tell him about this secret cave.' Carrying Batty, she darted back down the passage to the open air. She knew that George had the ability to swim and breathe under water. The power he acquired the first time they travelled through the Rainbow Cave had been useful before and he could use it now to escape from the Robes.

'You must tell George where we are,' said Milly to Batty. 'Tell him to swim into the waterfall.' And she threw the bird into the air.

After Milly re-entered the passageway, the Polly tree straightened up and spread its branches out again to hide the secret opening. Inside the cave, Milly joined Singer and Tatu staring out through the curtain of water. They were able to see Batty land on the roof of the cabin next to George, but then the boat got caught in the current of the waterfall and was sucked violently into the torrent of falling water. They could only watch helplessly as the boat disintegrated. Bits of wood splintered off and somersaulted through the air before sinking into the churning water. The front of the boat disappeared in the raging torrent and, for a moment, the back of the boat tilted upright in the air before being hammered out of sight by the force of the water.

The watching children gasped in horror at the sudden destruction of the boat. They hoped George had been able to escape overboard before disaster struck.

It seemed an eternity before George suddenly burst out of the water right in front of them and heaved himself up into the cave. For a moment he sat exhausted on the stone floor hardly able to speak.

Milly and Singer clapped their hands with delight and immediately hugged him.

'My word!' he said as he climbed to his feet. 'That was some waterfall. If I hadn't been able to breathe down there, I would never have survived. Thank goodness for the Rainbow Cave and its strange gifts.'

'Charlie has a gift,' said Milly, smiling happily at George. 'But he's not too happy with it.'

'Oh yes, what is it?'

'He can speak any language and communicate with all sorts of creatures, even without speaking. It's amazing.'

George looked around the cave, 'Where is he?' he asked.

The girls stopped smiling. 'The Snakeheads have captured him,' said Singer gravely.

'We have to go and rescue him,' added Milly. 'And soon. We don't know where they are taking him or what they will do with him. But the horses are following him and they will help us.'

'And so will the Jambucks,' added Singer. Then she turned to Tatu and said to George, 'This is Tatu, he's a Jambuck, but he can only talk with Charlie.'

George looked confused, so Milly told him all about the Snakeheads and the pit and how Singer and the horses had rescued her, but had to leave Charlie behind.

'We must go and help him, of course,' said George. 'But first we need to know what the Robes are doing.'

'I'm the only one who can do that,' said Singer quietly, 'and I'm the only one who can walk into the Snakeheads' camp and cut Charlie loose. You need to stay here for now, while I go and see what the Robes are up to.' Without waiting for a reply Singer called out, 'Be invisible!' Immediately she disappeared and they heard her walk down the passage towards the Polly tree guarding the entrance.

As soon as she left, Tatu took Milly's arm and pulled her to the back of the cave. In the corner she saw some steps had been carved into the stone wall which led up to an opening in the roof. To one side of the steps a small stream of water trickled its way down into the cave and out to join the waterfall. Tatu used sign language to indicate that he wanted her and George to take the steps.

'It must lead to the land above the waterfall,' she said excitedly to George. 'Once we've found Charlie, we can go and look for the Waterlanders. Tatu knows we are looking for them and now he's showing us the way to the land where they live.'

A noise at the entrance to the cave alerted them to Singer's return and they hurried to meet her. Batty was perched on her head.

'You can't lose me you know,' said the Tick-Tock bird. 'I was waiting for the tree to open up again.

'The Robes are everywhere,' said Singer in despair. 'They know we are hiding somewhere and Old Barking Mad is roaring at them, saying nobody leaves until we are found.'

'But we have to go and find Charlie,' said George. 'Perhaps we can slip by them?'

'I can,' said Singer, 'but only on my own. You would be caught and that wouldn't help Charlie.'

Tatu pushed George and Milly to the steps at the back of the Cave, then he turned round and taking Singer's hand he led her back towards the entrance. Then he stopped and nodded his head.

'Tatu wants us to go to the land of the Waterlanders and he wants to take Singer to look for Charlie,' suggested Milly.

'Tatu's right,' said Singer. 'I'm the only one who can get past the Robes and Snakeheads. You two should go up the steps. Charlie and I will follow just as soon as we can. Leave us a trail so we don't get lost.'

There was silence while Milly and George looked at each other and thought desperately of another way to rescue Charlie, but they both knew there was no other option.

'All right,' said George reluctantly. 'We'll start looking for the diamonds. You go and get Charlie back.'

'Take Batty with you,' added Milly. 'She's a good scout.'

Once Singer, Batty and Tatu had departed, George and Milly took a moment to assess the situation.

'I wish they had Drago with them; he'd show those lizards a thing or two.'

George gave a smile. 'You're right there.'

Milly's face became serious and she grasped George's wrist firmly, squeezing so much it almost hurt.

'Do you think he's all right, out there all alone on the grasslands, surrounded by those horrible sheep?'

George pulled away gently. 'Careful, Milly!' he said, rubbing his wrist. 'You might snap my arm.'

'Sorry,' she replied. 'Don't know my own strength...'

George placed a hand on her shoulder.

'Don't worry about Drago,' he said. 'He'll be fine. I'm sure of it.'

7

CHARLIE'S GIFT

The rope around his neck rubbed against his skin and made Charlie feel sore and uncomfortable. He was a prisoner of the Snakeheads and could do nothing about it.

As he trudged across the thick, wet terrain of the swamplands, he cast a few sideways glances at his fellow prisoner. He also had a rope around his neck and an expression of total despair. He was short, just a little bigger than Charlie, with pale green skin and thick, dark hair. The only item of clothing he wore was a loin cloth around his waist. On the couple of occasions that Charlie tried to speak to him, the Snakehead at the other end of his rope would jerk it forward to make him stumble, so they proceeded along in silence. Once the young man put out a hand to help him when he tripped and Charlie noticed his fingers were webbed like a duck's foot.

After hours of trudging, the sky began to darken and the Snakeheads decided to stop for the night. The prisoners were tied to a tree and given some boiled potatoes and porridge to eat. A Snakehead came over and stared at them for a moment, then kicked Charlie's foot.

'You will be useful to us,' he hissed in the strange

language of the Snakeheads.

'Why?' Charlie hissed back. His green companion looked at him with interest. He had never before met anyone able to speak the Snakeheads language.

'Because you can speak the same tongue as the Robes, and we are going to trade with them, so we won't eat you just yet.' The Snakehead cackled with amusement, then turned his attention to the other prisoner. 'This creature however has brought us diamonds and is now only good for pulling carts and hard work.'

With a slithery hiss, the Snakehead stomped away and the two prisoners were left alone. If they whispered, the Snakeheads were far enough away not to hear them. The webbed man spoke first. He talked in a new language, but Charlie understood him immediately and was able to reply.

'Where are you from?' the man asked.

'From a land behind the great thorn hedge,' replied Charlie, trying to make it sound as grand as he could. The green man looked confused; he'd obviously never heard of the *Great Thorn Hedge*.

'How can you speak our language and the language of the Snakeheads?'

This was too complicated for Charlie to explain in detail, so he simply said, 'It's a gift.' There was a brief moment of silence between them, before Charlie asked, 'Why did you bring diamonds to these creatures? Where did the diamonds come from? Why are you a prisoner as well?'

The man took a deep breath before giving his

reply.

'We dig the diamonds out of the ground and take them to the men in orange robes who use them in a great building called the Dome. They want more and more, so we do a lot of trade with them. To get to the land of the orange men, we have to cross the swamps.' He tried to use his hand to gesture to the wide open meadow, but his wrists were bound too tightly. 'We were ambushed by the Snakeheads and I was captured. Unfortunately, I was the one carrying the diamonds, so now the Snakeheads have them, and plan to steal our trade.'

'What is your name?' asked Charlie.

'Bredon, son of Akbar,' the green man answered, lifting his head proudly. 'My father is the chief of the Waterlanders.'

'So you're a Waterlander,' said Charlie. 'I thought so. We came looking for you.'

The Waterlander looked at Charlie and gave a thin smile. 'Looking for diamonds too, I suppose.

Charlie looked down, suddenly feeling quite ashamed. Was his quest for diamonds any different to that of the Robes, or even the Snakeheads?

'What do the Snakeheads want diamonds for?' he asked at last.

'To trade with the orange men of course, but they will ask for weapons. They will get spears and swords and axes. The orange men will trade with anyone for diamonds; they won't care that arming the Snakeheads will mean death for a lot of other creatures, perhaps all of us... We Waterlanders may never be able to leave our Waterlands again, for fear of the Snakeheads.'

They talked a lot that night and Charlie learned that the Waterlanders lived on a high plateau above the waterfall, reached only by a secret path up the mountain. In the Waterlands the rivers and lakes teemed with fish which provided the people there with ample food. That, thought Charlie, accounted for the webbed hands of his new friend.

'We need to escape,' said Charlie, 'and get the diamonds back.'

Bredon shook his head sadly. 'Nobody ever escapes from the Snakeheads. You become a slave, then they eat you.'

'I have friends,' said Charlie with a smile. 'They will free me.'

Bredon gave a resigned shrug.

'I hope you're right, my friend. I hope you're right...'

Throughout the next day, Charlie and Bredon struggled to pull a cart along through the forest. They had little time or strength to talk and although Charlie kept a sharp eye out for his friends, there was no sign of them.

He'd seen Singer release Milly the day before, and allowed himself a quiet cheer when the two girls and the Jambuck had fled into the forest, but as each hour passed, his concern grew that the others would not be able to find him again and he would succumb to the terrible fate that Bredon had come to accept as inevitable. Still, he was sure Singer would do everything she could to get help and return, and when she did, they must also rescue Bredon and recover the diamonds.

The only sign of life in the meadowlands was a solitary white horse that appeared every now and then throughout the day. Charlie watched it closely and dared to hope it was following them.

That evening, when they stopped for the night, Charlie whispered to Bredon.

'Where are the diamonds?'

'In a white leather pouch tied around the waist of one of the Snakeheads,' came the reply.

'Which one?'

'One of the big ones I think, but I don't know which.'

Just before dark, two things happened. A tick-tocking noise came from a tree just above them; Charlie jerked his head up to see Batty settling down on a branch. As he stared at her she opened one eye and winked at him. Then, the white horse appeared and led a number of other horses close to the camp where they stopped, apparently grazing.

Charlie nudged the dozing Bredon gently in the ribs

'Stand by,' he warned, 'and don't be surprised at anything you see,'

Moments later a knife appeared in front of them, floating in mid-air. As Bredon watched, startled, the knife sliced away at the rope binding Charlie to the tree. Bredon tried to pull away, fearing some dark power, but Charlie hissed at him.

'Don't move, it's only my friend, Singer. She's here to rescue us, like I said.'

The knife cut through the rope holding Charlie and he was free. Then, at his signal, the knife moved over and began to cut Bredon's ropes too.

'Singer,' hissed Charlie as quietly as he could. 'We need the diamonds that are in a white pouch around one of the Snakeheads' waist.'

'All right. Leave it to me.' The reply was a faint whisper. Charlie knew Singer was nervous and frightened, but he also knew her courage.

'Wait until you see me reappear then run like mad to the horses,' she said, as soon as Bredon's ropes were severed.

It seemed an eternity before they saw a large Snakehead jump to his feet and lumber about, still half asleep. He snarled and hissed loudly before starting to chase after a small, white bag that flew through the air and away back across the meadowlands. In the gathering gloom, the Snakehead tripped over some of his sleeping companions. Startled awake, they jumped to their feet as well, roaring and spluttering.

'Be visible,' the shout came from Singer and she ran towards the distant white horse who immediately came racing to meet her.

Total confusion engulfed the camp as Charlie and Bredon leapt away from the tree they had been tied to and darted past the bewildered Snakeheads. They had a good start and followed Singer in a mad dash across the meadow to where the other horses were waiting for them.

In a great slithering shuffle, the Snakeheads gave chase, their flat feet pounding on the heavy ground.

Singer, driven by fear, leapt onto the white horse's back and threw her arms around its neck. As soon as it felt she was secure, the horse turned and galloped away.

Two other horses arrived and clattered to a stop. Bredon and Charlie jumped onto their backs and moments later were following Singer towards some more horses standing a good distance away. When they reached them, Charlie saw that the other horses carried Jambucks who were all clapping their little hands together to celebrate the escape of their new friends.

Tatu greeted Charlie with a cheerful whistle, the strange language of the Jambucks.

'I am glad to see you again. We have never known anyone like you! The horses know a way that leads to the high lands where you can meet with your friends, and I'm sure this Waterlander will guide you to your destination.' Tatu gestured to Bredon, who sat astride his horse with a comfort born of skill and gave them both a curt nod of agreement.

'I am eternally in your debt,' said Bredon bowing his head, then flashing his teeth in a broad smile.

Singer handed him the white sack of diamonds. 'These are yours, I believe.'

'I thank you kindly; we need them to trade with the orange men.'

'Perhaps you could show us where you get them from, as we also would like to take some back with us.'

'Indeed I will, but it takes much time and hard digging to acquire such an amount,' said the Waterlander. 'But we need to travel to my land in the mountains before we can do anything else.'

'We left our friends in a cave under the waterfall. Tatu showed us the path to your land,' said Singer.

'That is indeed one of the secret ways,' agreed Bredon.

'The Robes were looking for us everywhere when I left.' Singer was nervous and her face wore a worried frown as she spoke.

'We will proceed with caution, but they won't find the secret entrance to the cave, I'm sure of that,' smiled Bredon. 'The orange men are big, noisy creatures with little sense. There is no doubt that with the help of your incredible gifts, we can slip past them.' He gazed at Singer with admiration as he spoke. She gave him a warm smile in return.

It was a long ride and they took it at a steady pace so as not to tire the horses, but before long they were back in more familiar territory.

By the time they reached the path to the cave, the horses were worn out and Singer and Charlie were aching with the effort of riding. During the journey Charlie and Tatu rode alongside each other and Singer could hear them whistling back and forth to each other, frequently bursting into high pitched laughter.

'We live amongst the trees at the edge of the forest,' Tatu was saying in response to one of Charlie's questions. 'As out of sight of the Snakeheads as we can be. The Snakeheads don't like the forest, but they can run fast so we have to be careful when we venture out onto the meadowlands.'

'It must help that the horses let you ride them,' said Charlie.

'It does, but we help them a lot with all sorts of tasks. Horses don't have hands like we have, so they can't tie knots in rope or carry things or remove stones that get stuck in their hooves. They are always nearby when we graze in the meadowlands and, if danger is close, we all escape together.'

'Sounds like a good plan,' said Charlie, nodding.

'It works,' Tatu answered with a sigh. 'Mostly...'

Upon arrival at the path through the forest, Tatu said, 'This is as far as the horses can go. We must proceed on foot to the cave now.' Charlie translated for Singer.

'We will remain nearby,' said the white horse. 'If the Tick-Tock bird is still with you when you return, she can fly and warn us that you are coming.'

At that moment an exhausted Batty landed on Charlie's shoulder. She had been flying as fast as she could to keep up with the horses and now she was puffing heavily with all the effort. 'Can we rest soon?' she asked in a very weak voice. 'I've never flown this much in my whole life!'

'Soon Batty,' Charlie reassured her. 'Just as soon as we find George and Milly and get to a safe place.'

Quietly they tiptoed down the path. Charlie held Tatu's hand and Batty sat silently on his shoulder. Singer became invisible and walked ahead of them with her eyes and ears alert for any sign of an attack from the Robes.

When she came to the Polly tree that guarded the entrance to the cave she stopped and let out a strangled cry of shock. In front of her, the Polly tree lay on its side with half its roots pulled out of the ground. The entrance to the cave was clearly visible.

Charlie ran up to join her and went straight to the Polly tree. 'What happened?' he grunted in Polly tree language.

'The Robes found out about my job here,' groaned the poor tree and Charlie heard its pain. 'They hacked and pulled at me until my roots came out of the ground, then they all rushed into the cave and they haven't come out since.'

Charlie translated for the other two.

'Impossible! They have found the path to the Waterlands!' cried Bredon in despair. 'We must hurry and warn my people.'

'We must help the Polly tree first,' said Singer, bending down to comfort the distressed tree.

'Tell your friend not to fuss,' said the tree to Charlie. 'I will feel better in a while, then I'll wiggle my roots back into the ground. But, not here, I'm afraid the secret of the path is lost forever.'

Charlie stroked one of the Polly's leaves and,

seething with anger, stood up to face the others.

'The Polly tree says to carry on,' he said. 'We can't let the Robes catch George and Milly or reach the Waterlands.'

Bredon led the way into the cave, running up the steps that led to the Waterlands with an agile familiarity.

'Take care, Bredon,' shouted Singer after him. 'The Robes might catch you.'

But Bredon was worried about his people and raced up the steps and out of sight. Charlie and Singer finally caught up with him as he waited impatiently on a mound outside the cave exit.

'Welcome to our land!' he said waving an arm across the panorama of lakes, mountains and forests.

Charlie looked out, astounded by the breathtaking view before him, and took a lungful of fresh mountain air. It felt good, but something still bothered him.

'Where are the Robes?'

Singer turned to Batty, who was still perched on Charlie's head, and said, 'Go on, Batty, fly high and find the Robes.'

The bird fluttered a little and looked as if she would refuse, but finally puffed out her chest as much as she could. 'I'll do my best,' she said. 'But if you see me drop like a stone, don't be surprised - just catch me.'

With that, she fluttered off, flapping her wings heavily. As soon as the bird reached a good height, she circled around a couple of times, then suddenly dived down towards them. Again she settled on

Charlie's head.

'Got them,' she announced triumphantly, pointing an outstretched wing along the side of the lake.

'About twenty Robes are walking round the lake on the eastern shore.'

'My village is on the other side of the lake,' said Bredon. 'The orange men are heading there. We must hurry around the western side and get there before them. It is a faster route, if you know how to go.'

'Then lead on,' said Charlie, keen to give the Waterlander all the support he could. 'We haven't a moment to lose!'

8

THE WATERLANDERS

After Singer and Tatu had left the cave to rescue Charlie from the Snakeheads, George and Milly had climbed the steps up to the Waterlands. At the top, another Polly tree covered the way out and, when they appeared, it obligingly leaned over to let them through.

Right in front of them a calm lake reflected the light so brilliantly, they had to shield their eyes from the glare. Squinting against the light, the pair of them scanned the landscape for signs of life.

'There,' said George pointing to some wisps of smoke floating skywards on the far side of the water.

'I see it,' said Milly. 'That must be where the Waterlanders live. But it looks like a long walk around the lake.'

'Wait a minute, there's a boat. Look again.'

It was hard to spot in the shimmering light and Milly strained her eyes to see a small boat bobbing on the water.

'It's not far out,' said George, 'and it seems to be empty. I'll swim out there and see if there is anybody on board. They might need our help, but in any case, if it's empty, we can use it to cross the lake. You wait here.'

Keen to use his powers again, George didn't hesitate to dive into the lake and swim out to the vessel.

Left alone on the lakeside, Milly found herself feeling reasonably safe for the first time in a long while. Selecting a soft and dry looking patch of ground, she was about to sit down for a well-earned rest when her peace was shattered by a strange whistling noise that grew steadily louder. It came from above, but before she could even look up, there was a loud cry of *Yoweeeee!* and a large object crashed into the lake.

It landed so close that water splashed all over her, making her jump backwards with surprise. Dripping wet, she stared at the ever-widening ripples where the object had submerged. As she stared, a shape broke the surface and rose up before her. She blinked, and saw the face of a boy staring at her through water-filled goggles, a look of complete surprise on his face. Long, straight hair flopped down to his shoulders and two rather large ears poked their way through it and stuck out sideways. Two hands reached up to raise the goggles and clear them of water. A broad smile stretched from ear to ear, revealing a gap in the middle of his front teeth. Milly could not help but respond to the infectious grin with a smile.

This boy needs a haircut, she thought, but the incongruous sight of the toothy grin on a boy peeping out of a lake in the middle of nowhere made her laugh. It must have been the release of tension because Milly could not stop laughing. The boy laughed with her and nearly choked as he slipped back under the water.

When he resurfaced again, he called out in a loud, high pitched voice, 'HELLO THERE,' and started to walk out of the lake. He was tall with spindly legs and dressed in ill-fitting red trousers and a black jacket which poured water back into the lake as he came towards her. On his back he wore a strange metal rucksack that had two tubes pointing out at the top and the bottom and a lever of some sort on one side.

'Hello,' he said again but much quieter this time. 'I'm Tod Beanpole. So pleased to meet you! I haven't seen a normal person for ages.' He held out a hand as he reached her and, gingerly, Milly shook it.

'I'm Milly,' she said. 'Where did you come from? And what on earth is that *thing* strapped to your back?'

Tod Beanpole flopped down onto the bank next to her. 'I need a rest,' he announced. 'That was a bigger crash than usual. I think I was going a bit too fast.'

'Where did you come from?' asked Milly again.

'From that mountain,' he pointed vaguely off into the distance. 'I live up thereabouts, and when I saw two normal people appear from nowhere, I just had to pop down and investigate.'

'You flew through the air?'

The boy struggled to unstrap his rucksack and showed it to her. 'I did, and this,' he added proudly, 'is a flying machine.'

'But there is no such thing as a flying machine. Where did you get it and how does it work?' asked Milly as she studied the strange contraption.

'I have no idea how it works,' the boy admitted with a shrug. 'I just pull this lever.' Tod touched the small lever at the side of the rucksack. 'It hums loudly for a few moments then *whoosh!* up it goes and I go with it. Have you heard of a place called the Dome?' he asked.

'Oh yes, I know it well,' Milly replied and she sat down next to him.

'Well,' he said. 'I used to work in the dome...'

Milly frowned. 'You're one of the orphans? I don't recognise you.'

She was trying hard to remember if she had seen him before, but how could she have forgotten a face so distinct?

'You know the Robes too then?' asked Tod, quickly.

Milly nodded. 'I know the Robes,' she said grimly.

'Well, there was an escape, you see. A lot of children got away.'

'I know,' Milly couldn't resist a little smile. 'I heard about that.'

'Afterwards,' Tod continued, 'there was a lot of commotion and the like, so I thought I'd escape too.'

Milly raised an eyebrow. 'You escaped from the Dome all on your own? How?'

'I sneaked into a room that nobody used and

hid behind a big, old wardrobe. The Robes looked everywhere for me, but I kept very quiet. After a while they went away and I wondered what to do next. Then I noticed that behind me, covered in cobwebs, was a door that looked as if it had never been opened, at least, not for ages. The handle turned and the door creaked open just wide enough for me to squeeze through. Behind it, steps went down a passageway, so, I went down too.' Tod, warming to his tale, lowered his voice and shifted a little closer to Milly.

'I was in a part of the Dome where nobody had been for years. There were cobwebs and thick dust everywhere. It was a bit frightening,' he confided, 'but very exciting at the same time. In one of the rooms I came across a pile of these things and I wondered what they were.'

He showed Milly the metal rucksack again and touched the lever gently. 'I pulled this up on one of them and it made an almighty humming noise. When I let go, it shot across the room, battered into one wall, bounced off it and crashed into another. I had to dive for cover. When it finally stopped crashing about, it lay on the ground all broken up. I thought it must be a rocket of some sort, and with the straps on it was surely made to be worn. I immediately thought that if I could sneak out into the open air, then, with one of these things on my back, I could fly away and somehow get back home. Except that I don't have a home...'

Tod Beanpole paused for breath and, for a

moment, seemed lost in thought. 'In fact,' he said at last, 'even if I did have a home, I'm sure I wouldn't be able to get there!'

'I have no idea what you mean,' said Milly, shaking her head. 'But tell me what happened next?'

'I strapped on one of the rocket rucksacks and tried to sneak out into the open. Unfortunately, one of the Robes saw me and set off such a racket, I had to run up some stairs to escape. Then more Robes joined the chase and I kept running up stairs until I got to the roof. I rushed out of a door and found myself on the roof of the Dome, trapped with nowhere to run. Just before the Robes could grab me, I decided to take my chances and pulled the lever.'

Milly was transfixed by the exciting story.

'Then what?' she asked eagerly.

'*Whoosh!* I shot straight up into the air,' Tod paused for a moment, smiling as he remembered his first journey.

'Go on,' said Milly impatiently, at the same time looking out across the lake to see if George had reached the boat. There was no sign of him and she was beginning to feel concerned. Tod Beanpole carried on with his story, almost talking to himself now.

'Fantastic,' he grinned again from ear to ear and Milly noticed a slightly mad look in his eyes. 'I shot up into the air, away from the clutches of the Robes and the Dome. I could see for miles and I flew in a great arc towards the mountains.' He stopped grinning for a moment, then added, 'Unfortunately I didn't know how to come down. I just blasted through the air until I remembered the lever, but when I pulled it down, the machine just stopped, and I landed with a bit of a bump, to say the least. Luckily, it was a soft mountain meadow, so the damage wasn't too bad.' He rubbed at an elbow, as though remembering the pain.

'It's all right flying up into the mountains. I can push the little lever down to make it stop, but unless I can crash in the mountains or down here into the shallow water of a lake, it's very dangerous.'

Milly stared at him in amazement. 'I'm surprised you're still alive.

Tod just laughed. 'So am I, and under these clothes there are bruises all over my body.'

'You must be the only person in the whole world ever to fly like a bird,' said Milly as she stared at the strange rucksack.

'Not so much like a bird,' said Tod ruefully. 'More like a crazy, out of control, rocket boy. Creatures of all sorts run when they see me coming.'

'I don't blame them. I wish I had seen you coming, you gave me such a shock.' She examined the rucksack. 'Can't you slow down at all? You just crash land every time?'

'Yes,' said Tod cheerfully. 'Don't touch that lever,' he added suddenly, as Milly examined the incredible machine in detail.

Two metal tubes, about three feet long, ran through a silver coloured metal box fixed together with heavy rivets. This box was mounted on a curved metal base, with straps on the other side. On one side of the box was the lever Tod had pointed to. On the other a small dial, with numbers around it.

'What's this dial for?' she asked Tod, who frowned at it and shrugged.

'No idea,' he said.

Lifting the rucksack, Milly turned it upside down and peered inside the tubes, but there was nothing to be seen except a hole with a series of metal rings around it. Tod looked on anxiously as she turned the dial on the side.

'Look,' she said, turning the rucksack towards him. 'When I turn the dial, the hole inside gets narrower. Maybe that would help to slow you down when flying through the air.'

Tod peered down the tubes as well and gasped. 'Goodness! What a clever thing you are!' he cried. 'I must try it immediately.'

A noise from out on the lake distracted them. Looking up they saw two people sitting in the boat and starting up an engine.

'The Waterlanders are fishing,' said Tod. 'They live on fish and they're always out on the lake or swimming under the surface. They have webbed hands and feet, you know... Very odd...'

'But where is George?' cried Milly, shielding her eyes to watch the Waterlanders steer the boat away from them.

'George who?' asked Tod, strapping the rocket pack onto his back.

'The boy I was with earlier. He was going to look at the boat.'

Tod shook his head. 'No idea,' he said, grasping the lever. 'Are you ready for this?'

When George dived into the water, he took his time swimming to the boat. Strange coloured fish darted in all directions and he stopped frequently to marvel at them. Some of them came right up and stared curiously at him from close range. Along the bottom of the lake, large shellfish snapped their shells shut as he glided over them.

Up ahead, the hull of the boat came into view. Putting on a spurt he swam strongly onwards when out of nowhere a heavy net wrapped itself around him, along with all the nearby fish. Within seconds he was completely tangled up in it. The more he struggled, the worse it got; the strands of the net were too strong to break and as it was pulled towards the boat, the net got tighter and tighter. When he realised the boat was now pulling the net along under the water and he was part of a catch, he gave up struggling. He remembered that the Waterlanders were fishermen and they were most likely pulling their haul of fish back to land.

He thought of reaching for the knife in his pocket and cutting himself free, but unable to move either arm, he knew this was hopeless. There being nothing else he could do, he resigned himself to his plight and let the net carry him along.

'Where is he?' repeated Milly looking out over the lake. 'He should have reached the boat by now; he's a very strong swimmer.'

'The Waterlanders set nets under the water and then throw bait overboard. When all the fish swarm in to eat it they pull up the net quickly and tow it back to their village over there.' Tod pointed to the wisp of smoke on the other side of the lake and then his eyes opened wide with a sudden realization. 'Oh dear, your friend may be caught up in the net. He'll be drowned. I must go and help him.'

'No,' said Milly calmly. 'He'll be all right, he has this power; he can breathe under water. We'll just walk round the lake and meet up with him on the other side.'

'How can anyone breathe under water? That's highly unusual,' said Tod, scratching at his wet, matted hair.

'You can fly,' said Milly. 'That's quite unusual too. Now let's get round this lake.'

Tod Beanpole picked up his rucksack and turned it a few times. 'The straps are long enough to fasten two people onto this rocket machine. We can cross the lake and be at the Waterlanders village before George gets there.'

Milly looked at him in horror and again she noticed a mad gleam in his eyes. 'You are crackers,' she said. 'I'm not flying anywhere, especially with you.'

'Please,' said Tod, 'this rucksack is too heavy for

me to carry very far, so I have to fly and you'll be walking round the lake on your own if you don't fly with me. Then you'll have to spend the night out in the open, and there are strange creatures that come out at night. I often hear them howling.'

Milly didn't know what to do. If she was honest with herself, the idea of flying over the lake, like a bird, was quite exciting to say the least.

'Let me show you how I go up,' said Tod hopefully. 'And, if twisting the tubes works, maybe I can get down again without crashing,'

Milly agreed and Tod strapped on the rucksack. 'Look,' he said, holding out the straps. 'If you stand in front of me these straps are long enough to stretch around you and hold you tightly. You'll be quite safe in the air.'

'It's the crash landing I'm worried about,' responded Milly, as she stood back and glared at him. 'Go on, fly and show me it's safe.'

Tod smiled happily and, standing up straight, he pulled the lever on his rucksack. Immediately the machine hummed loudly, then, with a loud roar, it quivered from side to side before lifting slowly off the ground with Tod dangling from the straps.

'Look, its easy,' he laughed. *Whoosh!* The flying machine shot up into the air and Milly could hear his cackling laughter fade away.

She craned her head backwards to watch Tod flying above her then she saw his hand bend around his back and twist at the tubes. For a moment he hovered in the air, then dropped like a stone. Milly leapt backwards to avoid the inevitable crash. But with some frantic twisting of the tubes Tod managed to control the rucksack and, after jerking around in the air backwards and forwards and up and down, he finally managed to land only a few metres away from her.

'Fantastic!' he shouted with delight. 'Brilliant, I can control it beautifully. Come on, strap in!'

Milly was being cautious. 'I don't know,' she said doubtfully. 'It still looks very dangerous.'

'You'll be fine,' insisted Tod and again he grinned broadly. 'Come on, we'll cross the lake in no time at all.'

Reluctantly, Milly stood in front of Tod and allowed him to strap both of them into the rucksack.

'Ready?' he asked

Too frightened to speak, Milly just nodded and closed her eyes. When Tod pulled the lever, the machine hummed loudly again and Milly felt herself lifted off the ground and suspended from the straps, which now bit deeply into her waist and shoulders. When she opened her eyes and found herself dangling over the lake, she screamed.

She was still screaming when they passed over the boat. The two Waterlanders looked up and Milly could see the surprise on their faces. Behind the boat she could see the faint outline of the net being towed along. Eventually she stopped screaming and looked around her. There was the mountain where Tod lived on one side of the lake and she could see meadowlands and forests with more lakes and mountains in the distance. As the flight seemed to be under control, she allowed herself to relax a bit and look around some more. Soon the Waterlanders' village came into view.

'I don't know the Waterlanders very well,' confided Tod, leaning forward and shouting in Milly's ear. 'They run around screaming whenever I fly over them, and of course, I can't speak their language. I just hope they are friendly.'

'Now you tell me!' Milly cried. 'I thought you knew them!'

'Oh no! Actually I often sneak into their village to borrow things. You know, food and wood and what-have-you. They sometimes see me but never try to stop me. I think they are frightened of the flying machine.'

'I don't blame them,' said Milly. 'So am I.'

Below, a crowd of Waterlanders had gathered at the water's edge. Behind them, several huts formed a wide semicircle around a larger hut in the middle. The huts were made of wood with layers of grass on the roofs. Tod twisted the tubes on the rucksack and hovered over the village for a moment, then slowly he began to descend.

All the Waterlanders were staring up at them. Milly could see that the men wore narrow loin cloths and the women were dressed in patchwork leather gowns tied at the waist. There were a lot more women than men, and lots of children of all ages staring up as well. The blue waters of the lake and the yellow sand together with the pale green skin of the people combined with a variety of multicoloured cloth made a vibrant scene.

When it became obvious that Tod and Milly were about to land, the crowd scattered in every direction. Milly was dangling just below Tod and she watched fearfully as the ground came up to meet her. Just as it seemed a safe landing was possible, Tod pushed the lever down and the machine stopped about two metres short, then dropped down. Milly crashed into the sand by the lake, with Tod landing heavily on top of her.

The breath was knocked out of her and she felt sure she'd broken an ankle.

'That was a dreadful landing,' she shouted at Tod. 'Will you please get off me?'

Although Milly broke Tod's fall, he toppled over backwards and knocked his head hard on the ground. Clearly dazed, he did his best to get to his feet, but the extra weight of Milly held him down and they both lurched to one side.

A young Waterlander girl overcame her fear of the crazy rocket boy and rushed across the sand to help. She was smaller than Milly and her leather dress was dyed a bright yellow. Her pretty face was full of concern as she kneeled down behind Tod and, pulling at his rucksack, she tried to lift him to a sitting position.

Milly smiled at her and started to undo the straps that held her tightly to Tod. 'Mind that lever,' she warned the young Waterlander as the girl pushed at the rucksack.

It was obvious that the girl didn't understand Milly, because she slid her hands up the sides of the rucksack to try and lift it.

'DON'T TOUCH THAT LEVER!' Milly cried again, and she twisted round to try and grab the girl's hand.

It was too late. The child had knocked the lever up and the humming started. Milly knew what was coming and screamed out, 'Pull the lever down!'

The girl still didn't understand what she was saying. Tod was still too groggy to know what was happening and, although Milly twisted and wriggled she couldn't reach the lever in time. The rocket took off, the Waterlander girl fell over backwards and Milly screamed again.

The Waterlanders had been approaching to help when the rucksack shot up into the air. Immediately they stopped in their tracks, turned around and ran away again to watch from a safe distance.

Out of control, the rocket raced through the air in a great arc, then headed up towards the nearby mountain. Tod was dangling from the straps of the rucksack like a rag doll, and Milly was hanging underneath suspended upsidedown by a strap still fastened round her waist.

'Tod, wake up,' she screamed.

But Tod was too dazed to understand the danger they were in. She could hear him singing loudly, *'Red switch, blue switch, old switch, new switch...'*

The rocket rucksack took them over the edge of the mountain in no time at all. Although she was dangling upsidedown, Milly could see a forest below them. Suddenly, the rocket started to come down at high speed heading for the mass of trees. Milly closed her eyes, covered her face with her hands, and waited for the crash, while Tod, oblivious to everything, carried on singing and waving his arms. '*Which switch the right switch? Which switch the wrong..?*' he trilled in a high-pitched voice.

They skidded into the canopy trees, which slowed them down a little. A branch knocked the lever into the down position; almost at once, the rocket engine stopped working.

The pair burst through the branches and crashed to the ground in a clearing. Struggling free, Milly felt herself all over and decided that apart from the bruised ankle she was, by some miracle, alive and well. She knew Tod was unharmed, because he was standing up, waving his arms and still singing loudly.

'*Press the right, what delight! Press the wrong, Ding Dong..!*'

'Will you shut up, you blithering fool!' she shouted, clenching her fists in rage and pondering whether or not it might be worth giving him a quick thwack around the jaw to snap him out of his delirium. She thought better of it and kept her fists by her side.

After wandering in circles for several minutes, Tod stopped and looked closely at Milly, who stood with her arms folded and a very grim expression on her face. Tod frowned. 'Who are you?' he asked.

Milly sighed in exasperation, but before she could say anything, Tod burst out laughing. 'You're Milly! I remember now, we flew over the lake. But, how did we get here?'

'We landed in the Waterlander village, then accidently took off again. We're lucky to be alive.' She glared at Tod, but he was staring past her, at something coming through the trees.

'Oh, dear,' he said in a small voice. 'Look Milly, warriors. This could turn out bad...'

She whirled round and saw Waterlanders circling and closing in on them. The warriors were very different to the others down in the village. These Waterlanders, all men, carried long, pointed spears and their faces were painted with bright colours. Although short in stature, like the rest of the Waterlanders, they looked fearsome and ready to fight. Broad-chested and muscular, each of them had his spear firmly planted on the ground in front of him with the sharp end pointing to the sky. Milly looked all around for a means of escape, but they were now completely surrounded.

One of the warriors stepped forward. He wore a red band of cloth around his head and, by the way the others all looked to him, was most likely their chief. To everyone's evident surprise, he raised his spear in the air and began to laugh loudly. As if by command, all the other men joined in. They roared and laughed and cheered and waved their spears wildly.

Milly and Tod gazed at them in astonishment,

until Tod's face broke into a toothy grin and he cheered as well. Raising his hands, he walked around the circle, encouraging the Waterlanders to continue their laughing and cheering.

'Hurrah!' roared Tod, although he had no idea why he was cheering.

'Hurrah!' howled the Waterlanders in reply.

'Do you know these people?' hissed Milly.

'Nope,' said Tod happily. 'I've seen them around, but we've never been properly introduced.'

The man with the headband seemed to be the leader. He came up to Tod with his arms outstretched and proceeded to enfold him in great big hug. Then the others crowded round, patted Tod on his back and shook his hand firmly over and over again.

'I say,' said a bewildered Tod, 'would you mind telling us what's going on?'

The lack of a common language didn't stop the Waterlanders talking to Tod in a very excitable manner. Even though he didn't understand a single word they were saying, he smiled and nodded and laughed heartily from time to time, as if he followed every sentence.

Totally ignored, Milly was gradually squeezed to the back of the crowd, then finally ejected from the circle altogether. She just had to watch while Tod was mobbed and treated like a hero. Suddenly they all dropped to their knees in front of him and bowed their heads to the ground.

Milly and Tod stared at each other over the heads of the bowing Waterlanders. 'Do they think you are some sort of a god?' wondered Milly, baffled at such a curious notion.

'It must be something to do with the flying machine,' Tod replied. 'They must have seen me flying and crashing all over the place.'

Standing up again, the chief put his arm round Tod's shoulders and led him off down a path through the forest, followed by the others, with Milly bringing up the rear, and left to carry the rocket pack by herself.

After a short walk they came to a clearing with a circle of tents, no doubt the base for the hunting party, and were installed on a pile of cushions and brought food and drink. After their meal, tired and thoroughly exhausted, the pair were led to another tent in which a pile of furs had been laid out to make comfortable beds for them. Then, with many smiles and a great deal of bowing, the Waterlanders departed from the tent and left them alone. With nothing else to do they settled down for a good night's sleep.

'Ah well,' said Tod, 'that seemed to work out well. It's been a good day.'

Although it was dark, Milly just knew he was beaming his toothy grin at her. 'You're mad!' she said. 'It has been a day of disaster. I've lost all my friends and found *you* instead. I do not call that a good day.'

9

UNDER ATTACK

The next morning they indicated to the Waterlanders that they had to go back down the mountain as soon as possible. The chief frowned but bowed politely to Tod, who bestowed his toothy smile on him. They were given a parcel containing food and drink (actually Milly was given the parcel, which a young man strapped tightly to her waist without saying a word). It was obvious that gods weren't expected to carry anything. However, when the chief brought out the rocket rucksack and tried to strap it onto her back, she protested loudly and Tod, smiling in a superior, godlike fashion, insisted that gods do sometimes carry things and that he would allow it to be strapped to his own back instead of the girl's. With the pack firmly in place, they were led to a path which led downhill in the direction they wanted to go.

It took an hour of scrambling downhill before they ran into the village and saw George standing amongst a group of Waterlanders and helping to pull in a net full of fish from the lake. As they ran towards him shouting, out of the trees on the other side of the village burst Charlie, Singer and Bredon also shouting at the top of their voices.

The joy of reunion was short lived as Charlie, short of breath from his long run, gasped out a warning. 'The Robes are coming around the other side of the lake. We need to act fast!'

Bredon translated the message to his own people, shouting in the Waterlander language. The women and children gathered together with the few men and clustered nervously around Bredon.

'I must hide my flying machine,' said Tod suddenly. 'I don't want the Robes to find it.'

The little Waterlander girl with the yellow skirt was already standing by him and, when he looked around for a hiding place, she took Tod's hand. She obviously liked the spindly boy with the friendly grin and was trying to pull him to a hut and out of harm's way.

'Go on!' shouted Milly. 'Go with her and hide the rucksack.'

Charlie, George and Singer stared at the retreating figure of Tod and turned to Milly with a quizzical look on each of their faces.

'Who's he?' asked George.

'*He* is *trouble*,' said Milly, curtly. 'He's from the Dome. His name is Tod Beanpole and I think he's a little insane, but harmless. I'll tell you about him later.'

Batty arrived and screeched loudly. The bird was hovering high above and keeping a lookout for the Robes. 'They're coming,' she shouted in her shrill voice.

As soon as the warning was given, a hoard

of Robes charged towards them. There was no mistaking the large figure of Jethro Barking, or the loud voice that roared with triumph when he saw the friends clustered together on the beach. The Waterlander women and small children ran to the huts for shelter. Only the few men remained.

Tod appeared alongside Milly and said bravely, 'Stand behind me, I'll protect you.' He was carrying a large stick which he shook at the Robes just as they responded to their leader's mad commands.

'Grab them! Tie them up! No Mercy!'

'NO!' shouted Milly pushing in front of Tod. 'I'll do the protecting, you just keep out of my way.'

It was going to be an uneven battle. Four Waterlander men and five children, of whom only Tod had found a weapon, matched against the bigger, stronger and well-armed Robes. The secret weapon was Milly. She stood crouched in front of the defenders with her arms outstretched, fists balled, ready for the fight.

The first Robe had obviously never seen Milly in action because he ignored her when he got close. Swinging a club, he tried to rush past her, but she landed a punch square in his stomach and stopped him in his tracks. All the breath knocked out of him, he let out a gurgled roar. With his arms clutching his waist, he toppled over and took no further part in the fight. The club he was carrying was picked up by George who used it effectively against a sneering Robe trying to grab him.

Milly hit out at every Robe she could reach, each

punch landing with a forceful crunch. By the time Jethro Barking panted up to the fight, it was going quite well for the defenders. The Waterlanders, especially Bredon, were using their fists pretty well, taking the lead from Milly and copying her skilful moves. George was using his club to good effect and Charlie was darting left and right, tipping up the attackers by grabbing their legs and then wriggling away before being captured. Tod swung his stick around, but his aim was not always so good. At least it kept the Robes away from him.

Batty circled overhead and shrieked with rage.

'You horrid orange maggots! You baggy bloused brigands! Leave my friends alone!' As one Robe crept up behind Milly, the angry bird swooped down and dug her claws into his hood and pulled it over his eyes. Milly, alerted to the danger, turned round and delivered a strong left hook to the jaw of the would-be attacker. He fell to the ground with a dull thud.

Singer had disappeared, but the shouts and squeals of the attacking Robes indicated that she was doing enough to keep the fight more or less going their way.

Together, they kept the Robes at bay until Old Barking Mad produced the large net that the Waterlanders had used to haul in the fish. Two Robes rushed at Milly, passing either side of her and out of range of her flailing fists. Between them they carried the net which they flung over her then pulled tight. Losing her footing, she fell and was soon entangled in the damp webbing. Tod Beanpole rushed forward to help her and he also got caught up in the net.

'Crazy boy!' she snarled when Tod's toes were accidently squashed into her mouth. As the Robes pulled the net tighter, Tod was somersaulted over the top and ended up lashed tightly to Milly, their faces so close they had to stare into each other's eyes.

'I told you to keep out of my way,' she hissed at him.

Tod grimaced. 'I thought you might need some help.'

By this time, George and Charlie had also been overpowered and were now being tied together by a pair of Robes. With the children trussed up and captured, the Waterlanders all darted into the lake to escape.

Jethro Barking let them go with a snort. He was more interested in the children from the orphanage. Though he knew the Waterlanders had diamonds somewhere, and he wanted them badly, he was pretty certain he'd be able to collect them later.

Milly had her hands firmly tied together before she was removed from the net and forced into the big central hut along with the others.

'Where is the lever to the hedge?' growled Jethro Barking as he towered over them, his hands resting on his wide hips. 'You must know or you wouldn't be here.' The orange hood lay flat on his shoulders and he glared at them with eyes like big, black buttons. His blotched face was redder than usual; the big man was very angry.

'I'll feed you to the sharks, hang you by your feet, give you to the Muttons one by one if you don't speak up!'

A Robe hurried into the hut. 'Master, we have found some diamonds,' he declared.

'Good!' snarled the King of the Robes and, after a look of pure hatred at Milly and George, he left the hut.

There was a movement at the back of the hut. They all turned round to see the little Waterlander girl in the yellow skirt poke up her head from behind a pile of rugs. She was frightened and had been crying.

Charlie immediately spoke to her in the Waterlander language. 'Don't cry,' he said. 'Just stay hidden and you'll be all right. What's your name?'

Her eyes opened wide with surprise, delighted at being able to speak to him.

'Samsa,' she said, 'and I can help cut your ropes.' She held up her hand and in it was a sharp looking knife. 'If my father was here, he would rescue us and scare off all those horrid orange creatures.'

'Where is he?' asked Charlie. 'But first, please cut these ropes.' He wriggled his wrists to show the little girl what he wanted her to do. Using her knife she cut his ropes in one slice. Tod was next and then she darted over to George and Milly.

'Be visible,' came a loud whisper and Singer

appeared in front of them. Her white dress looked even worse for wear, but she smiled happily and seemed in good spirits.

The little Waterlander girl squealed with fright when Singer suddenly appeared and Charlie had to put his arm round her shoulders and explain how clever Singer was at becoming invisible. Tod's eyes opened wide with astonishment and Milly told him about the power of the Rainbow Cave.

'You lot are amazing,' said Tod. 'I want to be changed as well. I want to fight like Milly.' He looked at the little girl with admiration.

Charlie glared at him. 'That's what I said, but all I got was the ability to talk to anybody. But...' he admitted, 'it is working out well. I'm getting used to it.'

George walked over to the Waterlander girl and put his hands on her shoulders. 'You said that your father could help you. Where is he?'

'He's in the forest on the mountain, hunting with the rest of the men,' she said eagerly, looking up at George. 'Shall I escape and run up the mountain to tell him about the attack?'

'We've met the warriors,' interrupted Milly. 'For some strange and unaccountable reason they think Tod Beanpole is a god!'

Tod pulled himself up to his full height and beamed at everyone. 'Very sensible people they are too. I have always suspected I was different to other children.'

'You certainly are!' said Milly, glaring at him.

'That's because you are crazy.'

'We need to escape very soon,' said George. 'You heard Old Barking Mad, he's going to torture us until we tell him how to get back through the hedge. We don't want him back at the orphanage or anywhere else in our world. What can we do? Think everybody!'

Singer was looking at a hole in the roof of the hut. It was obviously used for ventilation but was not very big. 'Do you think that hole is big enough for a rocket boy to get through?' she said thoughtfully.

They all craned their necks and stared at the hole.

'He does always go straight up in the air,' said Milly. 'We can position him right under the hole and shoot him out. I think that's a very good idea!'

'Right ho,' said Tod, 'except for one thing.'

All eyes looked at him puzzled.

'I don't have my pack.'

There were groans all round and a few sighs.

'I hid it somewhere, and in all the confusion, I forgot where.'

Without a word, the little Waterlander girl stepped forward and pulled back the blankets under which she had been hiding.

'Are you looking for this?' she asked Charlie, indicating the rocket pack that lay underneath.

'Ah,' cried Tod in delight. 'That's where I put it!'

Immediately, he struggled into the device and began to tighten the straps.

'Not on your own,' said Milly holding out a restraining arm. 'They might think you are a god, but you could do something crazy, and you can't speak the language. Take Charlie with you.'

'You're going to fire me out of that little hole strapped to that thing?' screeched Charlie, looking horrified.

'Yes,' snapped Milly, 'or would you rather be tortured by Old Barking Mad? You'll be quite safe; Tod sometimes steers in the right direction, and with your help, you should manage to find the Waterlander warriors.'

'But you said he always crash lands. If I'm dangling underneath him, he'll land on me!'

'Then you'll have to help him land properly.' Milly was unsympathetic and told him how to operate the tubes on the rucksack before pushing him towards the hole in the roof.

This time Tod was facing Charlie when they were strapped together. 'This way you can reach the tubes on the rucksack and help Tod to land,' explained George, as he tightened the final strap and carefully positioned the two rocket boys underneath the hole.

Standing back, they all watched with apprehension as Tod grinned at them and gave a short salute. They all saw the mad gleam in his eyes, even poor Charlie, who whimpered slightly.

'Let's go,' laughed Tod, and, without another word, he pulled the lever.

The rucksack quivered from side to side and hummed loudly. Charlie closed his eyes and covered his face with his hands. Rapidly the rucksack lifted off the ground, gathered speed and whooshed up through the hole and out of the hut, leaving behind a shower of broken twigs and scattered grass from the roof.

A cluster of orange hooded faces looked up, disturbed by the commotion, to see two boys strapped to a rocket and heading high into the sky.

By heaving on his straps and pushing out his arms, Tod was able to steer the rocket rucksack to where he thought he had last seen the Waterlander warriors. Beneath him, Charlie had his eyes clamped tightly shut and let out a long, terrified scream.

The lake sparkled as Tod steered their flight towards the forest on the mountain plateau. Very soon he spotted a clearing in the forest. As it was the only one he could see for miles around, he shouted instructions to Charlie and pointed down to the green space below.

'That's the place! We're going in!'

Without waiting for Charlie to respond, Tod shut off the lever and the two boys plummeted towards the ground. Daring to look, Charlie could see they were heading straight for the trees.

'No!' he shouted. 'Not yet, we're too high!'

Tod flipped the lever on again and the rucksack lurched upwards and rose again, twisting and spinning as they went. The clearing veered out of view, then came back in as Tod waved his arms about some more.

'Twist the tubes,' he ordered and Charlie reached up to give them a turn in an effort to slow the rocket down. They were so close to the trees that Charlie had to lift his legs as high as he could to avoid hitting the branches. 'Higher!' he shrieked.

But Tod was already braced for a landing as soon as the trees disappeared. The grassy clearing rushed up to meet them. With a rough jerk he twisted the tubes again, slowing the pack down a little more just before they hit the largest tent in the clearing.

They both screamed loudly as they tore into a tent and squashed it flat. Tod landed on top of Charlie and knocked all the breath out of him. Within moments, the Waterlanders appeared all around them and clapped their hands with delight.

'Get this crazy boy off me,' shouted Charlie in the Waterlander language. Then he felt someone wriggling round underneath him and realised that a Waterlander had been in the tent when they landed and helped to break their fall.

One of the applauding Waterlanders pointed at Charlie and spoke. 'This strange boy speaks our language, how amazing!' Then they rushed forward and lifted the two boys off the tent.

'Two crazy rocket boys,' said a Waterlander. 'How many more are there?'

'None,' said Charlie. 'There is only one crazy rocket boy and it's him!' He pointed at Tod who was smiling and nodding at his admirers.

A lump in the middle of the tent worked its way towards them. A bedraggled Waterlander with a red headband emerged looking dazed.

He glared at Tod. 'I knew it must be you. Who else flies through the air crashing everywhere?' For a minute it looked like Tod was about to lose his godlike status, at least in the eyes of the chief.

'We need help,' said Charlie in a serious voice. 'Your people in the village below have all dived into the lake to escape an attack by the Robes and my friends have been captured. A little girl called Samsa is with them.'

'That's my little girl!' said the chief in a horrified voice.

All the Waterlanders started shouting at once, bombarding Charlie with questions. 'Where's my wife?' said one. 'Has anyone been killed?' asked another.

Charlie held his hands up. 'I don't know,' he said. 'There was a fight, but I think your families escaped into the lake. Bredon is with them.'

'We must go!' the chief cried. 'At once!'

Grabbing their spears and clubs, the Waterlanders began to make their way down the mountain, leaving Charlie and Tod alone in the clearing.

While the Waterlanders were racing down the mountainside, the Robes were searching all the huts for diamonds. When they had finished, they dragged George, Milly and little Samsa out onto the lakeside.

'Come here, you green monsters,' Barking roared at the Waterlanders swimming like fish out in the lake. 'If you don't come ashore immediately, I'll chop this girl up like salad.' He held Samsa high in the air.

But he had not chosen his moment well, for behind him a band of enraged Waterlander warriors burst out of the forest after their rapid dash down the mountainside. With a mighty howl, they raced to the rescue of their friends and loved ones. The spears and the screams, the face-paint and the rage combined to render them a fearsome sight.

Old Barking Mad dropped Samsa onto the sand and stared at the rapidly approaching warriors in horror. He had always dealt with timid Waterlanders when trading with them previously; he hadn't realised there were also fierce warriors in their homeland.

His red, blotchy face turned white with terror as he tried to find a way to escape the approaching danger. Desperately he looked everywhere until he spotted the fishing boats bobbing up and down in the shallow waters at the edge of the lake.

'The boats!' he screeched. 'To the boats!' In a desperate attempt to take a prisoner with him, he made a grab at the nearest one, which happened to be Milly. Unfortunately for him, the invisible Singer was also standing nearby and, sticking out a foot, she tripped him up before his grasping hand could reach its intended prey.

Scrambling to his feet, the King of the Robes took one more look at the rapidly approaching warriors and decided to join the rest of his men in a rush for the boats. The engines started up and the boats turned towards the deeper waters of the lake. Since the web-footed Waterlanders could swim like fish, the warriors kept up their chase, plunging into the water fully intent on catching the Robes. But it was hard to use their weapons and swim at the same time, so after a few futile attempts to tip the boats over they had to give up. The Robes were also armed with spears and jabbed at the swimmers when they got within range, so after a while the boats sailed away to the far side of the lake and the Waterlanders returned to their shore.

'We must follow them round the lake!' cried Bredon, as the warriors gathered to discuss their next move. 'What if they return with reinforcements? That must not happen! Never again can the caves be used by the orange thieves!'

The chief then stepped forward into the circle and spoke.

'Bredon is right. And if the Snakeheads find the secret passage then our life here will be impossible,' Raising his spear high in the air, he shouted again, 'We must fight!'

The Waterlanders roared their approval and set off round the lake. George grabbed a spear from the ground and joined in. 'Down with the Robes!' he roared, racing to catch them up.

Milly tried to follow, but her ankle was too sore to run, so after a few paces she stopped and reluctantly watched George and the Waterlanders disappear into the distance.

When Charlie and Tod finally found their way back to the village, it was too late to join George in the chase after the Robes, so they joined Milly in the big hut and nursed their bruises.

Making their way along the lake's edge, George and the warriors could see the Robes' boats sailing straight across the water and heading for the secret path through the cave.

For a while they ran through dense forest and up a hill. When they came back down to the lake again, they saw that the Robes had already landed near the cave. Although the angry warriors sprinted the last few hundred metres, the Robes had disappeared into the cave by the time they arrived.

Exhausted, they collapsed in a circle by the entrance and George, who had struggled to keep up, joined them. 'Shall we follow them down into the valley?' he asked, gasping for breath.

'No!' said the chief. 'The passage is narrow and we'd be picked off one by one if we charge down.'

'We have to let them go,' panted Bredon. 'But we will make sure they don't come back this way.'

'How?' asked George.

'Follow me,' replied Bredon, and walked towards the lake where the waterfall cascaded down to cover the cave entrance far below them.

Two boulders set close together kept the water from overflowing into a trench that ran between them. George noticed that a great wooden gate had been fixed between the boulders and a long handle was attached to it.

The Waterlanders lined up alongside the handle

and on Bredon's command they all lifted it together.

'Stop!' he called out again. The gate had risen a short way and water immediately flowed along the trench and made its way to the entrance of the cave. The water swirled around the Polly tree and, to George's amazement, the tree leaned over backwards and pulled its roots out of the ground. Behind it, a little higher up the hill, some of the Waterlanders were jabbing their spears into the ground and loosening the soil. Swaying and wobbling, the Polly tree moved towards them. It lifted its roots high in the air and flopped them down in front of it. Then it swayed forwards dragging more roots behind it. When it reached the loose soil the roots disappeared into the ground in a flurry of flying earth as it wriggled and squirmed its way into its new resting place.

The Waterlanders, lining up behind the handle of the gate, watched the Polly tree settle down safely on high ground. As soon as it had stopped wriggling, they heaved the handle higher into the air. The gate opened wider and water from the lake poured into the trench with a great tumbling roar. It rushed, gurgling and splashing, into the entrance of the cave and flowed away into the darkness below.

'That will stop them ever using the path into our land again,' said Bredon with satisfaction.

'But how will you get down yourselves?' asked George, with concern. 'And how will we get home again?'

'There is another path down to the lowlands that

you can use, but for us, we have no desire to trade with those villains again, or face the Snakeheads. There are other tribes further north we can trade with, although it means a longer and more difficult journey, but they can also provide us with engines for our boats and cooking pots and other things made of metal.'

George was relieved to know there was a way down, but he felt a twinge of despair when he realised that the Robes had taken the Waterlanders' diamonds with them and that the journey home would take them through the Rainbow Cave. From now on, he was certain, the Robes would be guarding the Rainbow Cave in force. Old Barking Mad was not about to let another opportunity slip by.

Preoccupied with thoughts of the journey home and the many problems they would have to face, George felt a hand on his shoulder. Looking up, he saw Bredon standing beside him, his face serious and drawn.

'You came for diamonds as well,' said Bredon with a jerk of the head. 'But it will take time to dig for them. You could be staying with us for a while yet!'

10

DIAMONDS & PEARLS

Some of the Waterlanders took to the boats and sailed back across the lake while a dejected George and the rest walked back to the village. His spirits were raised a little when he saw the preparations being made for a feast to celebrate the arrival of the friends, the departure of the Robes and the safe release of Bredon.

Tables were brought out from the huts and soon they were laden with plates of delicious food. The main course of freshly fried fish was heaped up on plates for the four friends and they tucked in with relish. In fact, in all their lives, they had never had such a sumptuous meal.

When Singer took a final mouthful of the fish, she bit on something very hard and choked. Everyone turned to watch her with alarm, but when the offending object was retrieved from her mouth, she assured them she was fine and held up a small round pebble for all to see.

'A small stone in the fish,' she said. 'That's all.'

Bredon came over and took it off her. 'So sorry,' he said in his strange tongue. Charlie translated for him.

'It's a pebble white. The fish eat soft-shelled

creatures that live on the bottom of the lake and these pebbles are inside them. The fish usually spit them out, but sometimes we find them in our food.'

He drew back his arm and made to throw it away when George stopped him. 'Let me see that,' he gasped. 'It looks like a pearl!'

Taking it from Bredon's hand, George poured some water over it and polished it on his shirt. First, he held it up to the light then rolled it onto the table for all of them to see. It was white, perfectly round and, as the light reflected off its surface, rainbow colours shimmered from within its centre.

Singer gasped. 'It is a pearl and it's beautiful,' she said, picking it up gently and looking at it closely.

The chief, now known to all as Akbar, joined them. 'You can have as many of those as you like,' he said smiling. 'But you can't eat them and they are not much use for anything. When the cooks prepare a meal, they throw away any pebble whites, but, as Bredon said, mostly the fish spit them out before we catch them.'

'Oh no,' said Milly. 'Such a waste! We don't need diamonds if we can find more of these pearls; they are very valuable back home.' Her eyes sparkled as she smiled at Akbar.

Bredon laughed. 'After the meal I'll show you where you can find them. It's a lot easier to find pebble whites than diamonds, particularly as George has the ability to swim like a fish, because they are all underwater on the bottom of the lake.'

A great variety of fruits and cream cakes were

provided to finish off the meal, which the friends couldn't resist. While they were eating, they passed the pearl around and marvelled at it.

'This one alone must be worth a few bob,' said Singer. 'It's bigger than any I've seen in a shop window in London.'

'When Robert and I were selling the diamonds in London,' said Milly in an excited voice, 'all the jewellers had necklaces and broaches and bracelets made with pearls and they were very expensive.'

George stood up, clutching the edge of the table. His face had gone pale and he trembled a bit with excitement. 'Are there really more of these pebble whites under the water?' he asked Bredon.

'Oh yes,' Bredon replied. 'Lots! If you like really big ones, then the deeper the water the bigger they are. Come on, I'll show you.'

The friends crowded into a boat and with Bredon steering they sailed into the middle of the lake. Passing the tiller to Charlie, the Waterlander said, 'You steer the boat in small circles while George and I swim down to the bottom.' Then taking two bags he gave one to George and dived over the side. With hardly a splash he disappeared under the surface. Quickly, George followed suit and swam down out of sight.

Bredon was the first to return. After he surfaced he passed a bag up to Milly, before heaving himself back into the boat and gasping to regain his breath. Excitedly she opened it up and inside were three pebble whites, all about the same size as the first one, but dirty and half covered in algae and slime. Eagerly, the friends washed and polished the pebbles to reveal pearls that glistened with soft translucent colours playing across their surface.

It was a while before George's head broke the surface, but when he did, he was grinning from ear to ear and holding a bag high in the air. He passed it up to Milly; it was full of pebble whites. George clambered back into the boat and they all cheered and clapped him on the back.

'We don't need to go digging for diamonds,' he said, laughing. 'There are pearls all over the bottom of the lake. Not everywhere, but they are there if you look for them. Usually in small clumps and, Bredon is right, the deeper I went the bigger the pearl. It's fantastic.'

They stayed with the Waterlanders for several

days and made a lot of friends. Charlie was constantly in demand as a translator and the boys helped the Waterlanders with their fishing while the girls stayed in the village, cleaning and polishing the pearls that George collected. Finally, they had so many that the smaller ones were thrown back into the lake otherwise the bags would be too heavy to carry.

It was George who announced one morning that they needed to leave the Waterlands and start the journey home. Everyone went very quiet, suddenly aware of the dangers that lay ahead: the journey down the secret path to the land of the Snakeheads, the trip down river with no idea where to find a boat. But it was the trip through the Rainbow Cave that worried them most of all. The Robes would be waiting and they had no wish to fight with them again.

'I can guide you down the path,' said Akbar, 'and my warriors will escort you to the valley below. But we cannot go any further.'

'I can find the horses,' said Batty, who was perched nearby. 'They promised to carry you to the Rainbow Cave.'

'I wish there was some way of avoiding the Rainbow Cave,' groaned George, a frown etched upon his forehead.

'I want to go through the cave,' said Tod Beanpole with great enthusiasm. 'I have to get a power like the rest of you. I want to be a fighter!' He jumped up and danced around with nimble steps, jabbing his fists out and pretending to box.

'We can't climb the cliffs around the Rainbow Cave,' said Milly thoughtfully, 'but, maybe we can fly right over the mountain.'

They all looked at her in amazement. 'How can we do that?' asked Singer.

'Tod said he found a room full of rucksacks just like the one he has. He also said he was chased up to the roof and then flew away. We know the rocket rucksack can carry two people so, we just reverse the process. Tod carries one other person onto the roof of the Dome, then they sneak down to the room he found and bring three other rucksacks back to us.'

There was a long silence while they all thought about the plan.

'The Robes will see Tod when he flies in and all rush up to the roof of the Dome to capture him,' said Singer doubtfully.

'Not if he goes at night,' said George excitedly.

Charlie liked the idea of flying with his own rucksack. 'Then we can fly straight over the hedge,' he declared happily.

'I'm afraid not,' chipped in Tod. 'I've already tried it. There is an invisible barrier over the hedge, I bumped into it and bounced back. It made me crash land in amongst a pile of sheep. They seemed friendly at first; I thought they were smiling at me when they showed their teeth. But as they got nearer I noticed how sharp the teeth were and the vicious look in their eyes. I only just had time to fire off my rucksack before they attacked... I never went back.'

'It's a blessing Muttons can't fly...' said Milly grimly.

Early the next morning they set out on the journey back home. A band of warrior Waterlanders took them further up the mountain before taking a path that sloped sharply downhill. In addition to the pearls, they also had to carry supplies, so each had quite a heavy load.

At first they sang songs as they walked along, then they just chatted as the path descended lower and lower. Suddenly the Waterlanders came to a stop as the path seemed to go straight over the edge of a cliff.

'We can take you down as far as a bridge over the little wild river, after that you'll find the path that leads down to the plains,' said Bredon.

Akbar the chief nodded in agreement. 'Follow me,' he said and seemed to throw himself over the edge.

Gingerly the friends eased their way to the edge of the cliff and peered over.

'Oh my goodness!' exclaimed Singer.

Far below them the path snaked down a bare mountainside and disappeared into trees halfway down. Beyond the line of trees the meadowlands stretched out as far as they could see.

'Look!' said Charlie. 'There's an eagle!' Below them a large bird floated in the air, circling as its keen eyes scanned the ground for signs of prey.

'Don't like it, don't like it!' squawked Batty in alarm. 'Eagles and large birds with great big beaks like to eat Tick-Tock birds.'

They exchanged worried looks. When they reached the plains they were relying on Batty to find the horses.

'Come on!' called Bredon, who had followed Akbar.

With George leading the way, they went in single file down the steep path. Once Singer slipped and slid down past the others. She had to be hauled to her feet by Bredon, who was waiting for them to catch up. She was shaken and frightened, so after that progress was much slower.

By late afternoon they had reached the tree line and the forest began to grow thicker. It was a relief to have the support of the trees alongside the path, which gradually levelled out and made walking much easier. They could hear the noise of rapidly running water. 'It's the little wild river,' said Bredon cheerfully. 'You'll soon be down to the plains.'

A few moments later Akbar stopped and raised his hand. Bredon and the other Waterlanders all crowded round him. In front of them the noisy little river crashed and swirled its way down the mountainside. It was deep and fierce but quite narrow. A watery mist, thrown up by the torrent, splashed over their clothes and dampened their faces. Akbar turned to them with a look of horror on his face. 'The bridge!' he said. 'Its gone.'

A few wooden struts stuck out from either side of the bank, but the middle part had been wrenched out and swept away by the surging waters.

'But this is the only path!' said Bredon, looking up and down the river in despair.

As awkward as the situation might have been, it was also a chance to rest and so all of them removed their heavy packs and sat down. After a while, George suggested they walk along the bank to see if there was another way across the river further along. Only Charlie felt energetic enough to join him,so the two of them set off staying close to the river bank, struggling through thick undergrowth that tore at their clothes as they went.

'Wait!' said Charlie suddenly. 'I can hear a Polly tree talking.'

George watched as his friend furrowed up his brow and concentrated on listening to the low grunting noises.

'I can see you strange creatures. You must be the boy who can talk to us. All the Polly trees are watching out for you. Come and talk to me.'

'And me!' Charlie heard the grunts of another tree talking as well.

'Can you see a Polly tree anywhere?' asked Charlie looking around.

'No,' said George. He moved closer to the edge of the river with very cautious steps. In spite of the white plumes gushing over his feet, he took a few more steps forward, holding on fast to the nearest rock.

'There!' he said, pointing. 'In front of us, I can see some little yellow fruits of a Polly tree. Its branches are waving at us.'

Scrambling further down the riverbank, they came to a large Polly tree, whose waving branches spread out across the river. Charlie stared up at it. 'Can you help us?' he grunted.

'So delighted to meet you, strange boy. We Polly trees have been talking about you ever since we heard of your fight with the Snakeheads. We all want to help.'

'The bridge is broken and my friends and I need to cross the river,' said Charlie, staring into the branches of the tree.

'I believe my friend and I can be of assistance,' said the tree.

Charlie looked around and saw another Polly tree on the other side of the river waving its leaves at him.

'Come inside,' said the first tree, opening up its thorny branches.

Charlie and George stepped under the branches and into the hollow gap by the tree trunk. It was a larger tree than any they had met before and they had to look up to see the oval shaped head and its two lumpy eyes at the top of its trunk.

'Bring your friends and we Polly trees will help you cross the river.'

'How can you do that?' asked Charlie.

The Polly tree chuckled, a strange rasping noise. 'Can you hear me, brother?' it called. By way of reply, there came a series of loud grunts.

'I can, and I'm ready to help.'

'You had better leave now, my friends,' said the tree to Charlie. 'I am going to rearrange my branches.'

'Come on,' said Charlie to George. 'Somehow, the trees are going to help us cross the river. We have to fetch the others.'

They walked back along the river, stopping to stare back at the two trees. With a crackling noise the branches of the tree on the far side of the river straightened up and reached out over the water. The same thing happened to the tree they'd just left. When both the trees leaned out over the river their branches met and intertwined. Small, thin twigs wrapped around each other and pulled tight as larger branches flopped on top of each other to make it seem as if it were one tree with two trunks.

The boys stood and watched in amazement. 'Come on,' called out the nearest tree, 'we can't stand like this all day.'

Immediately Charlie turned round and, with George right behind him, raced back to the broken bridge.

'Quickly,' called out Charlie as he joined the girls and the Waterlanders. 'The Polly trees are magnificent. There are two of them by the river and they are keen to help us. You should see how they've leaned over the river and joined up their branches. But we have to hurry.'

In a few minutes they arrived back at the Polly

tree bridge and stared at the two trees.

'Come on. You need to climb up my trunk and when you reach my head please be gentle. Stand on it and just above me I have some thick branches you can use to cross the river. Hurry now, my branches are beginning to ache.'

Charlie translated and they hurried into the Polly tree. It was hard to clamber up the trunk, but the Waterlanders helped the children to climb on their backs and jump up to the branches.

George led the way and Charlie was the last to climb the trunk. Bredon stood up and called out to him as he edged out along the bridge. 'We will not come with you, this is as far as we can go. Good luck dear friends, and I do hope we will all meet again one day.'

Charlie looked down and waved to the Waterlanders. He felt sad that he would probably never see them again.

It was a perilous crossing. The water was flowing powerfully underneath them and spray from the noisy, crashing foam covered them as they edged their way across. Thick branches formed the bridge for their feet with smaller ones linked together as a hand rail. Although the two trees pulled as hard as they could to keep the bridge steady, it swayed like a pendulum when they were all on it together.

George reached the other side first and dropped down to the bottom of the second tree. A little while later it was Singer who jumped down and with a sigh of relief she landed in George's arms. Then

Milly swung down from a lower branch and when Charlie joined them they left the shelter of the Polly tree.

'Thank you so much,' said Charlie as he turned round to face the two trees and grunted his message to them.

'All Polly trees will try to help,' came back the reply. 'Good luck and keep away from the Snakeheads!'

It was almost dark by the time they reached the end of the path and emerged from the trees. Standing at the edge of the plains, they looked around for the horses. There was no sign of them, so George climbed a tree and stared at the horizon. 'Nothing,' he called down. 'I'm afraid we need Batty to fly high and look for them.'

'I think it is too late this evening. We really need to find some shelter for the night,' said Singer. 'And I think there are too many eagles around for Batty to fly anywhere at the moment. Perhaps in the morning it will be safer for her.'

'We might as well spend the night here,' suggested Charlie.

'If we do, I'm sleeping with my rocket rucksack firmly strapped on,' said Tod with a gulp as he looked nervously around him. 'I've heard strange howling noises at night and you never know what creatures roam around in the dark.'

There was a rustle in one of the nearby trees and, looking up, they saw a large bird settling in the top branches. A green glow emanated from the feathers on its body like an eerie torch. A long neck, supporting a small bald head bent down and glowing eyes stared at them. Its savage looking beak was curved and claws were spread out at the end of short, stubby legs.

'Yikes! What's that?' yelped Batty and she jumped off Charlie's head and tried to scrabble down into his shirt.

'A night vulture!' said Milly grimly. 'We've met them before.'

'There are more of them,' said Singer pointing into the sky, where the birds were circling above them.

'Polly trees, we need more Polly trees,' said George. 'Can you hear any of them grunting?' he looked at Charlie hopefully.

'No, we must spread out and find some.'

It was only a few minutes before Singer called out from a little way back in the forest. 'Charlie, come here, I've found a Polly tree.'

Charlie and the others joined her and the tree spoke to him. 'I'm so glad you found me, I was hoping you would pass by. Can I be of assistance?'

'We need shelter for the night,' Charlie grunted.

'There are five of you, I will need help. Some more trees are nearby. Wave your branches brothers and let our Snakefighter friends know where you are.'

Charlie saw branches waving from trees all around them. He went to each Polly tree in turn, spoke kindly to it and offered his hand for a leaf to stroke. Before it was completely dark, each one of the friends settled down for the night inside the protective branches of their very own Polly tree.

The night vultures, having lost their prey amongst the tangled thorns, took to the air and departed in search of an easier catch.

II

MORE ROCKETS

The next morning, having taken their leave of the Polly trees, they gathered at the edge of the forest.

'We need to see if there's any danger out there,' said George, looking pointedly at Batty. She trembled in Singer's arms.

'Batty,' George continued in a softer voice, 'the vultures only come out at night. It should be fairly safe for you take a quick look.'

'I don't like the way you said *fairly*!' Batty retorted, snuggling deeper into Singer's protective embrace.

'Please, Batty. Just a quick look.'

With a sigh, Batty raised herself up and gave a few flaps of her wings.

'If I don't come back, send a search party...' she grumbled, and took off into the air. Minutes later she returned, her face grim. 'I can't see any horses,' she said, 'but there is a pack of Snakeheads heading this way along the edge of the forest.'

The news caused great consternation and the children looked at each other in horror. 'Looks like it's back to the Polly trees again!' said Charlie with concern.

'We might have to; the Snakeheads can run faster

than we can,' said George grimly.

'But we might not see the horses if they come looking for us,' said Singer. 'I'll climb a tree, become invisible, and watch out for them.'

George helped Singer climb a suitable tree and settled her down on a big branch with Batty on her knee. Before he had even got back to the ground, Singer called out.

'I see them, I see the horses! They're coming towards us, but so are the Snakeheads.'

George quickly climbed back up to join the excited girl. She pointed to a cloud of dust coming straight towards them from the middle of the plains. 'There are the horses,' she said. Then, she pointed along the line of trees where the Snakeheads were racing towards them. 'And there are the Snakeheads,' she added.

'They seem to know exactly where we are,' said George. 'That's strange.'

'Come on, everyone,' called out Singer. 'We have to run to the horses or the Snakeheads will get here first.'

George and Singer scrambled down as fast as they could. The group gathered their bags together and set off in a mad dash to the plain. Batty took to the air again, all fear forgotten, and flew ahead of them, screeching at the horses. 'Come on, this way, hurry, hurry!'

The horses changed direction slightly when they heard Batty and saw the friends racing towards them. There was a roar from the Snakeheads who also changed direction to cut off the running children. The horses ran faster. The Snakeheads ran faster. The children ran faster and the race was on.

One of the horses, with a Jambuck on its back, veered off towards the Snakeheads. With head down and hooves pounding the grass, the brave horse ran straight at the Snakeheads and charged in amongst them. The Jambuck carried a stick which he whirled round his head, whacking the Snakeheads that got too close. Some of them fell over and tripped up those behind them, forcing the hindmost to stop running. For a moment there was chaos amongst the scaly beasts, which allowed the other horses to reach the friends in good time.

As the galloping horses skidded to a stop, the children each ran to the nearest one and scrambled onto its back. Without wasting any time, the horses galloped back onto the plain. They didn't stop until there was a safe distance between them and the Snakeheads.

When the brave horse and the Jambuck caught up with them, the children cheered loudly and clapped their hands in delight. The Jambuck was Tatu and he was smiling all over his face.

'How did you know where to find us?' asked George. He spoke to the big white horse which was panting and covered in sweat after its mad dash to rescue them.

'We were looking out for you,' came the answer, 'and when your little friend surfaced this morning, we saw her. Unfortunately, the Snakeheads must have seen her too.'

'Thank you so much,' said Charlie on behalf of all of them. 'We met the Waterlanders and our mission is complete.' He held up the bag of pearls to show what he meant.

'Can you take us as near to the Dome as possible?' asked George. The horses had been such a help he didn't like to ask even more of them, but he needn't have worried. The white horse nodded his head and indicated that they should start their journey straight away.

Turning towards the east, the party set off at a strong gallop.

It took most of the day and by the time the group arrived at the top of the last hill, they were tired and aching all over from their long ride.

'This is as far as we can go,' said the white horse.

The Dome loomed large in the distance and behind it the mountains stretched in a great circle.

The children dismounted and each thanked their own horse. Translating for the group, Charlie thanked Tatu and promised to one day return the favour in what ever way he could. Then, with a snort and a stamp of hooves, the horses whirled round and galloped away.

When the sound of their pounding hooves had faded into the distance, George turned to Tod.

'When it gets dark, do you think you can land on top of the Dome?

'I'll need some help,' Tod replied with his toothy

grin. 'But yes, as long as there aren't any Robes guarding the roof, and as long as they haven't found the lost room behind the wardrobe.'

They needed a hiding place to shelter until dark. A copse of trees not too far away seemed the ideal spot so the five children settled down in the middle of it to wait for nightfall.

'Right,' said George. 'When it's dark, Tod will strap me into his rucksack and together we'll fly to the Dome.'

'No, I want to go with Tod!' said Charlie.

'I'm the biggest,' retorted George, 'and when we come back I'll have to carry two rucksacks as well as the one on my back. We have to have five rocket rucksacks to fly up to the mountains. Tod says that for long journeys we need one each.'

'Tod, if there are guards on top of the roof when you land,' said Milly, with a sweet smile, 'who would you like to have with you? An underwater swimmer like George? A translator like Charlie? Or a fighter like me?'

Milly knew the answer, and it only took Tod a moment to reply. 'You,' he said emphatically and gazed at her with admiration. 'I can't wait to go through the Rainbow Cave.'

There was silence; they all knew that Milly was right, but it was not easy for the boys to let a small girl go on such a dangerous mission. With a resigned shrug of their shoulders, they reluctantly agreed.

'Tod,' said Singer, putting a hand on the young man's arm. 'We aren't going through the Rainbow

Cave.'

Tod's smile faded and he was about to argue, but George raised a hand to stop him.

'Singer's right,' he said. 'The Robes will have the cave blocked and guarded. Our plan is to use the rocket rucksacks to fly *over* the mountains. First we fly to the river at the point where it comes out of the cave and then we follow it until we come to where it flows through Market Town. That brings us near to the gate in the hedge as we can get.'

'That's right,' agreed Charlie. 'We won't meet any Robes and we can go straight home. Once we have a rucksack each, it'll be easy.'

'What about Drago? We need to find him too, before we leave this place,' said Milly.

'Who's Drago?' asked Tod.

'He's our dog,' said Singer. 'We lost him when we arrived.'

'Not a good place to bring a dog.'

'He's not just any dog,' said Milly firmly. 'He's special.'

'And we'll do all we can to find him,' added George.

Tod frowned, stood up and walked up the hill. When he came back he looked thoughtful. 'There is a slight problem,' he said. 'Unfortunately, the rucksacks won't fly that far in one go. We'll have to stop somewhere on the way. I think the top of the cliffs near the cave is the best spot. The rucksacks need some time to recharge. They just stop when they run out of energy, which is awkward if you're up there!' He pointed a bony finger at the sky. 'Once you stop, they have to recharge themselves and they won't start up again until they are ready.'

'How long does that take?' asked George.

'I don't know. It varies. If they start, they're okay to fly, but they won't start if they have to go into charge mode.'

George nodded. 'Then we'll have to break our journey at some point.' he said. 'Let's hope it's not the wrong point...'

Darkness fell, sweeping over the land like the shadow of a giant hand. Having rested a little after their long ride, the group gathered at the top of the hill to prepare for their next challenge.

After helping Tod and Milly into the rocket rucksack, George, Charlie and Singer gave them a big hug, wished them all the luck in the world, then stepped back. Tod pulled the lever on the rucksack and immediately it hummed and quivered before lifting off the ground. Then, as the energy built up, it whooshed up into the air.

The brightly lit Dome was an easy target and, with Tod steering in his usual way of waving his arms and pulling on the straps, they wobbled to a position high over the Dome. Below them was the flat part of the roof that Tod had escaped from before. He pointed it out to Milly. 'We're going down now, hang on.'

Twisting the dial on the rucksack slowed them down. For the first time ever, Tod stopped the rocket at the right moment and landed on the roof with only a minor clunk. Milly fell over but didn't hurt herself and immediately started to undo the straps that fastened her to Tod.

As soon as she was free, she spun round ready for action in case any guards surprised them. But all was quiet apart from the usual drone from within the Dome. It came from the engine which provided the energy needed by the Robes to power their horseless carriages, boat engines, lights and all the rest.

'Follow me,' said Tod and, leaving his rucksack on the roof, strode towards the door that led down into the Dome and grasped the handle.

The door opened quietly and the two of them tiptoed down the stairs to a corridor which led to another set of stairs. Tod paused for a moment to try to remember how many flights of stairs there were.

'Four,' he said finally. 'Or is it five?'

'Make up your mind,' hissed Milly.

'Just follow me.'

After four flights of stairs, Tod selected a door and peeped inside. Turning to Milly he grinned from ear to ear. 'This is it,' he said, 'come on.'

Milly closed the door quietly behind them and helped Tod move a large, heavy wardrobe in the corner of the room. Behind it was Tod's hidden door. Opening it, he led Milly down some dusty stairs to the room where he had found the rucksacks. It was just as Tod had described, full of cobwebs, dust and dirt, with rocket rucksacks on shelves or just lying about on the floor, as though abandoned in haste.

'Let's not waste any time,' said Milly. Picking up the nearest rucksack she fastened it on her back. Tod did the same and, carrying a spare one each, they retraced their steps back to the stairs.

Milly peeped through the door to see if the way was clear for their escape and found herself staring at an orange gown. She came up to the chest of a burly Robe who grabbed her under the arms and lifted her level with his head. For a moment they stared at each other. Milly saw a pale, gaunt face with black eyes and short dark hair.

'The king will be delighted to meet you...' he said with a thin-lipped grin.

He didn't get any further. He had thoughtlessly lifted Milly to a most convenient position for her to punch him. She only had to draw back her arm a little way, clench her fist, and at lightning speed hit the Robe on the jaw. He let go of her immediately and fell in a crumpled heap to the floor. Milly picked up the spare rucksack she'd dropped and stepped over him. Tod followed and they ran down the corridor to the staircase.

A shout echoed from somewhere nearby, but they didn't stop to find out where, they just ran for safety. As they reached the stairs another Robe was climbing up from below. When he saw them, he gave chase taking the steps two at a time. They fled to the roof with Milly in the lead. More shouts followed them.

It took two flights of stairs for the Robe to catch up with Tod, even though the boy was running up the steps faster than he thought himself able. Near the top, he felt a big hand clutch his ankle.

'Yow!' he shrieked in fright as he crashed down on the hard metal step.

Milly turned and, dropping her rucksack, ran to Tod's aid. Using her foot she kicked the assailant in the chest and the unfortunate Robe turned a backward somersault and tumbled down the stairs.

More Robes now joined in the chase. In his haste to keep up with Milly and get to the roof, Tod dropped his spare rucksack. Milly turned when she heard the clatter of the rucksack on the stairs and called out to Tod, who was about to try and get it back. 'Leave it!' she yelled. 'You'll get caught, come on!'

The lost rucksack clattered down the stairs, halting the Robes' progress for a few valuable seconds. By the time they had moved it to one side and resumed their chase, the children had gained some precious distance. Gasping for breath, Tod and Milly burst through the door and onto the roof. Tod grabbed his old rucksack from where he'd left it and, clutching it to his chest, he pulled the lever on the rucksack on his back.

Milly crossed her fingers and, hoping her rucksack would start as well, she pulled the lever. For a moment they both hovered just above the ground before Tod's rocket burst out with energy and swept him into the air. He screamed with excitement as he rose above the Robes just as they poured out onto the roof.

Milly's rocket did the same a few seconds later. She also screamed with delight as she looked down and watched the Robes shake angry fists at them.

The Robes saw them fly straight into the air but didn't know which direction they took. Tod stared hard into the darkness and managed to pick out the silhouette of the hill where the others were waiting.

A crash landing was inevitable in the darkness and when George, Charlie and Singer saw Tod approaching rapidly, they scattered. It was just as well, because he hit the top of the hill with a bang and a shriek, then bounced back into the air. When he came down again the spare rocket rucksack went rolling down the hill and Tod went tumbling after it.

Milly dropped her spare rucksack before she landed in order to twist the rocket dial to slow her down. She was lucky because the slope of the hill meant she was able to roll down it instead of smashing into it. Finally Tod and Milly ended up at the bottom of the hill in a crumpled heap with their rucksacks still on their backs. The others gathered up the spare rucksacks and helped the two of them to their feet.

'Are you all right?' asked an anxious Singer.

Tod prodded himself all over. 'I am indeed and the mission is accomplished.'

Milly satisfied herself that all she had suffered were minor bruises before she pronounced that she also had survived the journey. 'Apart from Tod dropping his spare rucksack, we landed all right, found the correct room, fought off the Robes and escaped.'

'Well done,' said George, delighted that they had extra rockets and everyone was safe and sound.

They trudged over to the copse of trees and settled down to wait for morning and decide their next course of action.

'Can we manage with four rucksacks and five people?' George asked Tod.

'Not in one journey,' he replied. 'We have to get to the top of the cliffs, and we also have supplies and each of us is carrying a bag of pearls. It's too risky to take two people in one rucksack. I wouldn't like to crash land up there on those jagged rocks.'

'We'll have to make two journeys then,' decided Charlie. 'I'll wait here and when you four are safely on the mountain, Tod can bring a rucksack back to me.'

'Then,' added Milly, 'when we all get to the top of the cliffs, we can do the same thing on the journey down to the hedge.'

It seemed the only thing to do but George was not convinced. 'We'll have to wait until it is daylight to be able to see where we are going and when we take off, the Robes will be watching and they know there are five of us. By the time Tod gets back for Charlie, the Robes will be all over this hill. No, that won't do at all.'

'The Robes don't know about my power,' said Singer. 'If I am the one left behind, then it won't matter. I'll stay invisible until I see Tod coming back and become visible right at the last moment.'

They knew Singer was right so they settled down to wait for daybreak. Nobody even tried to get any sleep; they were all too excited at the thought of getting back to Mercy Hall with the pearls and meeting their friends again.

THE CROWN

Singer was already invisible when the four rocket children stood at the top of the hill waiting for dawn to show them the mountains. Their rucksacks were firmly strapped on their backs and their supplies and bags of pearls were strapped to their chests.

'Please don't drop anything,' said Milly. She was tense with excitement and very nervous. 'Especially the pearls; we need to sell them for enough money to keep Mercy Hall going for ever.'

George pointed to the cliff face which was becoming visible far away in the distance. 'There it is. Remember, we go in single file and follow me.' He pulled the lever on the rucksack and hovered for a few moments just a little way off the ground. Then Milly started her rockets, followed by Charlie and finally Tod.

Whoosh! They flew into the air, banked sharply to the left and headed off for the cliffs. Singer waved as they shrank into the distance.

Once they had slipped from view, Singer looked across at the Dome. George had been right; the Robes were waiting, ready to start a search for the children. She heard a roar go up as the flying rockets passed over them. Then watched as the

Robes started running towards the hill. She smiled to herself and sat down to wait.

The plan had been to fly in a tidy procession to the top of the cliffs, but George and Charlie had never flown a rocket rucksack before and found steering difficult. George thought he was going too fast so he twisted the rocket tubes to slow down. It made him drop suddenly as he passed over the Dome and he desperately twisted the tubes again to speed up. He immediately shot up in the air so fast he left his tummy behind and thought he was going to be sick.

Milly was lucky enough to point her rocket in the right direction. She soon took the lead and zoomed straight towards the top of the cliffs.

Charlie was even worse than George at steering. He suddenly dived down towards the ground, twisted the wrong tube and performed a complete somersault while screaming in fright. Just as he levelled out and found himself racing back towards the hill, Tod grabbed his arm and heaved him round to point in the right direction.

Milly arrived at the cliffs first. She picked out a spot on a broad plateau that gave them a view of the other side. Her landing was good - her best yet. She did fall over, but only gently. The other three finally arrived some time later with Tod holding George's arm in one hand and Charlie's arm in the other. All three crash-landed, but were unharmed and stood up on shaky legs to have a look around.

Below them they could see the river gushing

out of the Rainbow cave and winding its way to Market Town. Further on they saw the grasslands where they knew the dreaded Muttons lay asleep in their burrows. Behind them the hedge loomed and stretched as far as they could see. Above the hedge the light shimmered and became a shade of grey impossible to see through.

'That's where I tried to fly over,' said Tod pointing vaguely in front of him, then added, 'I must go and get Singer.' Picking up Charlie's rucksack he held it tightly to his chest and pulled the lever on his own rucksack. He flew in a great arc across the sky, hastening as fast as he could to the very top of the hill. Singer immediately became visible and ran over to him. While he waited for her to strap on her rocket, Tod waved to the Robes who were searching at the bottom of the hill. He pranced up and down, bowing and whistling insults at them. Enraged, the furious Robes ran faster up the hill driven by a desperate need to grab the sarcastic fellow and tear him limb from limb.

'Don't be so silly,' scolded Singer as she struggled to fasten the spare rucksack on her back. 'We need to get out of here!'

Tod grinned happily and helped her on with the rucksack. 'Hold my hand,' he said. 'We'll go together.'

He pulled the lever on Singer's rucksack.

Nothing happened.

The cocky grin vanished from Tod's face. Looking down, he saw the Robes were progressing rapidly up the hill.

'Uh oh...' he said, scratching his head with his boney finger.

'What's the matter?' asked Singer, eyes wide with alarm.

'Your rocket is recharging. Charlie must have used too much energy dancing around in the air. We'll just have to use mine, but I can't carry you *and* the rocket rucksack. Take it off, quickly.'

They fumbled at the catches and by the time they dropped the rucksack to the ground, the Robes were almost upon them. 'There's no time to strap you in,' said Tod in a panic.

Singer threw her arms around Tod's neck and he pulled the starting lever. The rucksack hummed as usual and they both sighed with relief. They seemed to hover for an eternity before it rose rapidly away from the Robes who were now racing towards them with their arms outstretched. Tod flung both his arms around Singer's waist to hold her tight and the rocket rucksack flew through the air towards the cliffs.

When he arrived, Tod dropped Singer into George's arms before landing himself. They were so relieved to see Singer safe and well that they hugged all the breath out of her.

'What now?' said Charlie, staring at the landscape.

'We wait,' said Tod. 'The rucksacks must all be charged before we take off again. I got the fright of my life when Singer's rocket wouldn't start, and because we had to leave it behind, now I'll have to bring two rucksacks back with me.'

'You know,' said Milly after they had waited a while, 'all Old Barking Mad has to do is drive along the hedge until he sees the marker we left behind to show where the square branch can be found. Then he's through the hedge and back home. He should have realised that we would have to leave something to help us find the right spot.'

'Maybe he has,' said George. 'I can see some of those carts without wheels gathering by the bridge. And there are a lot of Robes there as well.'

'Try the rockets,' said Charlie. 'If Old Barking Mad gets through the hedge before we do, then we will be the ones left behind in this land.'

They looked at each other in horror. 'That mustn't happen,' said Milly, now thoroughly alarmed at the thought of being stranded behind the hedge forever.

Tod, George and Milly grabbed their rocket rucksacks and, strapping them on quickly, started them up. To their relief, they all began to hum beautifully.

'We should fly in a straight line over the bridge!' called out George as one by one the rockets took to the sky.'

The Robes were just setting off in their carts when the rocket propelled children flew over them. On reaching the hedge, the children stopped as best they could. After George and Milly unstrapped their rucksacks, Tod grabbed them both and held on to them tightly. 'Don't leave without me,' he called out as he took to the air and headed back to the cliff top.

Charlie and Singer were dancing up and down with excitement and impatience when Tod returned. He dropped one of the rucksacks as he came into land at high speed and Charlie raced after it as it bounced along the edge of the plateau. Singer raced after Tod, who also bounced along the edge of the plateau in a particularly painful landing. He squealed, as his shoulder scraped along the ground.

Singer grabbed the spare rucksack and pulled it on. Painfully, Tod got to his feet and helped to strap her in. Pointing her in the right direction he started her rucksack and, after making sure Charlie was also airborne, he followed suit. Once again Charlie veered off in the wrong direction and Tod chased after him. Taking his hand he pulled him round and followed Singer towards the hedge.

Singer looked down at the ground below and saw Robes driving their carts as quickly as they could, whipping the little horses repeatedly and issuing harsh cries. The Muttons had been roused, and all over the grasslands they were emerging from their underground burrows and moving relentlessly towards the hedge, where George and Milly were waving wildly to attract their attention. The scarf was still in place and the waving was to tell them that the gate in the hedge had been found and they must hurry.

Something else caught Singer's eye. Turning her head she saw another creature racing across the grasslands, quickly passing the emerging Muttons and also heading in a straight line towards George and Milly. She stared at it very hard, fearful it might be a new and unexpected enemy come to join the fight. But then her heart gave a leap as she realised who it was.

'Look,' she cried out. 'It's Drago, he's safe!'

Moving like a speeding arrow, Drago raced across the ground to meet up with his friends. She shaded her eyes as light reflected off something on the dog's head and dazzled her. Drago seemed bigger than usual; she realised he was already angry and growing larger with each step.

Charlie mistimed his landing and shot over the hedge, only to hit the same invisible barrier Tod had discovered when he tried to fly over it. He bounced back, landed on top of the hedge and tumbled painfully to the ground.

The first of the pursuing carts arrived at the same time as Tod and Singer landed, both with a fairly chaotic bump. The Robes leapt out with a cheer and this time they carried spears. George heaved on the square branch and the hedge started to open.

Milly squared up to the Robes who sneered when they saw her. Singer struggled to her feet with the rucksack still on her back just as Drago arrived. In his mouth he carried the king's crown but when he saw his precious Milly facing the armed Robes, he didn't slow down but dropped the crown and launched himself at the enemy. Other Robes arrived but the gate was now fully open and George wanted the children to get straight through it. 'It only opens for a minute,' he screamed. 'Come on everybody, this way.'

The King of the Robes bellowed over the noise. 'Stop them,' his voice was a desperate howl as his cart came to a stop and he jumped out to join the fight.

The enraged dog now blocked the way for any Robe who attempted to pass through the hedge. Singer had hurt her leg and Tod dragged her through to the other side. Charlie was already through and Milly struggled after him as the hedge started to crackle and the branches started to bend. 'Come on Drago,' they all screamed together as they watched from the other side of the hedge.

The dog heard them calling and breaking off from the fight he darted through the hedge just as more and more Robes arrived.

Old Barking Mad roared with delight when he saw his crown lying on the ground and, momentarily distracted, he reached out to recover the symbol of his power.

But someone else had seen it too.

Before Barking's fingers could touch it, Batty swooped down and snatched it in her claws. Without stopping, she flapped furiously towards the closing hedge. Skimming the ground, she flitted through at the last moment, just missing the thorns and branches as they came together.

Drago also squeezed himself through in the final

minutes, but the closing branches snagged at his fur and he had to be pulled the last few feet by the children as the thorn gate snapped shut.

The Robes and their king remained stranded on the other side, their shouting cut off by the closing of the hedge. Safe on their side, the children could hear nothing but the peace and quiet of home. It was as though the strange lands beyond the hedge no longer existed.

They hugged each other and laughed with relief, but Milly was still anxious. 'Old Barking Mad knows where the square branch is now. The hedge could open up again at any moment,' she said in a worried voice.

George carried on laughing. 'After I opened the hedge, I removed the square branch and brought it with me. It's not real; it was simply screwed in,' he said holding up a branch of the hedge and waving it in the air. 'Nobody can get back here using the thorn gate.'

Drago returned to his normal size and stood panting while Batty lay exhausted on the ground with the crown still held firmly in her claws. Milly threw her arms round Drago and hugged him. 'You were magnificent!' she cried and then sobbed with relief. 'I'm so glad you found us.'

The children gathered round the dog and made a great fuss of him. 'What happened to you?' asked George. 'We thought you were going to be left behind.'

'When the log finally got washed ashore on this

side of the river,' said Drago, 'I decided to walk to the hedge very slowly, so as not to disturb the Muttons, and make my way to where I thought the gate might be. I hid in the nearby trees and watched for any sign of your return. When you all came flying through the air and crashed onto the ground, I couldn't believe my eyes.'

'We are so glad you are all right,' said Singer, patting the dog fondly on his head. 'We were so worried you had drowned.'

'And you brought the king's crown,' said Milly with delight. She picked it out of Batty's claws and placed it on her own head. 'Now I'm going to be the queen of Mercy Hall.' The crown was far too big for her and slipped round her neck.

'You can't be queen of Mercy Hall because it doesn't fit you,' said Singer laughing. 'Anyway it belongs to Batty now, so that means she is queen of the Tick-Tock birds, even if she is the only one on this side of the hedge.'

They could see the silhouette of Mercy Hall emerging from the gloom. Feeling tired but very pleased with themselves, they walked slowly along the path.

'You know,' said George as they approached the front gates, 'Mercy Hall must be the only house in the world that has a human fish boy and an invisible girl.'

'Not to mention the fastest runner in the world, an unbeatable girl fighter, and a boy who can talk in any language he likes,' added Milly.

'Don't forget the crazy rocket boy and a brave talking dog,' said Singer, putting her arm around Drago and giving him a hug.

'And a talking Tick-Tock bird,' added Batty, who was trying to keep her balance on George's shoulder.

'Yes,' said George, smiling, 'we're a strange lot to be sure...' Then his face dropped and he became quite serious. 'But I warn you,' he said, raising a finger to emphasise his point, 'what we are *must* remain *secret*, for *ever*, or we could lose everything. Is that understood?'

'Yes. Agreed. Understood,' said the others, one by one.

A cold mist was descending and a sudden chill came over them.

'Come on,' said George, pulling his jacket tight around him. 'Let's go home...'

EPILOGUE

'Stop it, you silly dog!'

The creature had been playing around his feet all day. All he wanted was to get on with sweeping the floor and making the whole place look nice and tidy for when his friends returned.

If they ever returned...

They'd been gone for some time now, too long for his liking, and he simply couldn't control the worry that gnawed at his insides from morning till night, and all through the night as well. The only way he could even begin to deal with it was to do what he knew he did best - sweep.

'Ruff!' cried Scruffy, pricking up an ear. He had heard something outside.

Scorpio thought he had heard it too. What was it? The patter of rain? The shatter of broken glass? Was another storm on the way?

There it was again, a delicate sound, floating on the air, like the sound of...

Laughter!

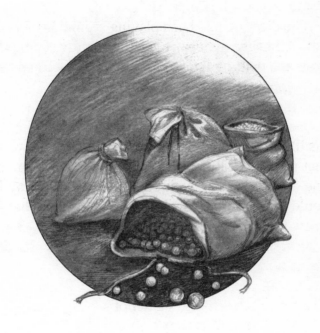

COMING SOON...

HEROES OF
MERCY
HALL

The final instalment

of

THE THORN GATE TRILOGY